HT '75
S

THE SHOOTING GALLERY

THE SHOOTING

Yūko Tsushima

Translated · and · compiled · by · Geraldine · Harcourt

GALLERY

PANTHEON · BOOKS · NEW · YORK

FIRST AMERICAN EDITION

Publication of this translation was assisted by a grant from the
Japan Foundation

Library of Congress Cataloging-in-Publication Data
Tsushima, Yūko.
The shooting gallery
Contents: A sensitive season—South wind—The silent traders—
The chrysanthemum beetle—Missing—The shooting gallery—
Clearing the thickets—An embrace.
1. Women—Japan—Fiction.   I. Title. II. Series.
PL862.S76A2   1988   895.6'35   87-22171
ISBN 0-394-56559-2
0-394-7543-2 (pbk.)

For Daimu

C O N T E N T S

THE SHOOTING GALLERY

A · SENSITIVE · SEASON

By this time the girl has almost passed out, but I catch her under the chin with my feet and begin to do the backstroke with my arms only, working extra hard to make up for the kicking part. Natchan is pacing up and down on shore, watching me and looking white as a sheet. I'm a powerful swimmer. The water splashing in my face makes a bright rainbow of colours. The sky is so blue you'd think it was painted with a thick coat of house paint. The girl, who was putting up such a struggle before, just trails like seaweed between my legs. She isn't heavy at all. Slowly the beach's sounds reach us. I hear Natchan's voice too: Come on! You can do it! I'm not a bit tired. In fact I put on a burst of speed and make it to the shore. As I'm about to lift the girl out of the water, Natchan throws her arms around me, crying, and tells me never mind about that, what a fright I gave her, took years off her life, what would she do if her precious Yutaka died? And she begs me never to do such a thing again. I answer impatiently: Do you think I could stand by and watch somebody drown? Besides, I'm the best swimmer in town. Don't make such a silly fuss, I tell her. Natchan gazes at me with red eyes and sighs. You've grown up, haven't you, Yutaka? And how tall you are. I smile at Natchan and run into the sea again. Natchan yells: Where are you going? I yell back: Come and have a swim. I'm not a bit tired. I could do another forty or fifty miles if I wanted. Natchan comes running shyly toward me in her white bathing suit . . .

'Don't you hear it, Natchan?'

His grandfather's voice breaking in popped the swelling sea-scape like a soap bubble, and Yutaka raised his sweatily glistening face and

1

sat up on the tatami. His body, the mats, the wooden posts of the old house, even the light out in the yard, all were sticky, as if oil globules hung in the very air. One mat's breadth away lay his grandfather, while his aunt was still doing the ironing in the corridor on the north side. Even their two shapes seemed to be shimmering on a surface of oil.

'. . . It's been going on all day.'

'What has?' asked Yutaka's aunt, not looking up from the ironing board.

'Listen, can't you hear it? That awful noise. It's coming closer.'

His grandfather was craning his thin, dark neck from his bed to stare into the yard as he spoke in an ominously hushed voice. Careful that the grown-ups didn't hear him, Yutaka let out a faint sigh, then after roughly wiping the sweat from his forehead and the end of his nose with his left arm he let his gaze fall on the plastic blocks scattered at his feet. There was a sort of truck bed nearly completed, which he'd intended as the foundations of a skyscraper. The building was to have been three colours – red, white, and blue. Taking it on his knees and dismantling it block by block, Yutaka began once again to entertain the doubt he'd almost forgotten beside the imaginary sea: wasn't Natchan going out? His aunt was so busy she was breathing hard, her arms were beaded with perspiration like fish scales, and yet she certainly didn't seem in any hurry. She looked all set to be ironing for another hour or two, as long as there was any laundry that needed it.

Before she began the ironing, Yutaka and his grandfather had watched together from their corner while his aunt did the laundry in the bathroom and put away the lunch dishes in the kitchen. The funny thing was that today his aunt showed no sign of going out.

Practically every day for the last month his aunt had piled the dirty dishes in the sink when lunch was over, changed into the blue jeans and cotton shirt she wore to go out, and hurried away as if dogs were snapping at her heels. She would arrive home at different hours, sometimes around four, sometimes after seven, but one thing was always the same: her eyes were red and her cheeks aglow like plastic balloons. She would come in the front door without a word, go through to the bathroom, take the wet bathing suit and towel from her

2

white basket and place them in the basin. While Yutaka and his grandfather were asleep she would rinse them out with care, changing the water often, and first thing the next morning they'd be out on the clothesline. That way they were thoroughly dry by noon.

Initially Yutaka and his grandfather had been at a loss to account for these new habits. They became so anxious that they took turns staying awake at night listening closely to her movements, and Yutaka even tried following her for some distance from the house – not too far or he'd get lost – but before long they'd begun to accept the change as evidently not a bad thing either for themselves or for her. Her colouring noticeably improved, her moodiness went away, and there wasn't the slightest trace of the violence that had made her pinch Yutaka's cheek for no reason or deliberately tread on her invalid father's feet. Yutaka and his grandfather had decided to allow Natchan these outings to the pool, but since it mattered that she be back in time for the evening meal they would act wistful when they saw her off and – at the risk of being thought outrageous hams – overjoyed at her return. Of course, this was essentially the grandfather's idea; Yutaka had mostly listened and nodded his approval.

—She's only twenty-six, you know – a mere child. At that age she still wants to have fun, and here she is, saddled with looking after an old man and a nephew. All things considered she's doing a pretty good job. You mustn't be too hard on her, Yutaka—.

—At twenty-six she's still a child, you know . . . It can't be helped . . . —

—Natchan'll grow up soon enough . . . —

Yutaka had nodded at these explanations, though he had a feeling his grandfather had said much the same back in the spring when they'd first learned of his aunt's friendship with the man from the building site next door.

Anything his grandfather had to say about his aunt was of interest to Yutaka, so much so that he'd pester him to go on, and he listened avidly to stories about his aunt and his mother when they were children or about himself when he was a baby. But there were days when his grandfather rambled on about his career at junior high school at such length that Yutaka couldn't get in a word about the events of his

3

day at school or his opinions of teachers and classmates, and on these occasions he quietly cursed the old windbag. They had always slept in the same room, living at such close quarters that his grandfather would notice a rip in Yutaka's shirt before his aunt did and each could guess how hungry the other was simply by looking at his face, yet Yutaka was becoming aware that this didn't necessarily add up to a liking for each other. He and his grandfather just happened both to be leaning on the same person. And both were treated by her as a nuisance. She disliked them. Still, it was more bearable to be disliked together than alone. His grandfather also taught him all kinds of things about the adult world. Yutaka had become knowledgeable on so many subjects that despite his bad grades he could just get by without being razzed by his classmates. He sometimes thought of his grandfather as a brother.

Yutaka and his grandfather quickly grew accustomed to his aunt's afternoon outings. She adhered firmly to her routine. And yet once lunch was over on this particular day his aunt had unhurriedly washed the dishes, showing no sign of ever getting ready. Yutaka and his grandfather had looked at each other quizzically: why didn't she go? It was his grandfather's theory that she couldn't be going to the pool alone but must be meeting that man she'd got to know during the construction work: then had they quarrelled the day before? She had stayed out unusually late, and when she still hadn't turned up by ten o'clock Yutaka and his grandfather had been reduced to nibbling on a couple of sausages with bowls of cold rice doused in hot green tea. Or did it simply suit the man to meet a little later today?

The aunt spent a good half-hour or more putting away the lunch things. When she came out of the kitchen the grandfather remarked to her, 'It's terribly hot again today, isn't it?' The aunt said without enthusiasm, over her shoulder, 'Yutaka, plug in the fan for Grandpa and don't point it toward his legs,' as she disappeared into the bathroom and turned on the water to fill the washing machine. Yutaka and his grandfather exchanged another look. Whatever could this mean? She'd already done one load that morning. It was hanging neatly on the line, from Yutaka's underpants to her own bathing suit. Yutaka felt vaguely alarmed. It had been almost midnight when his aunt finally arrived home last night. He and his grandfather had started out

4

of bed as the glass-paned front door rattled open, then just as quickly both lay down and pretended to be fast asleep. But his aunt made straight for her own room next to the kitchen, neither looking in at them nor stopping in the bathroom. At the sound of her door sliding shut, his grandfather had whispered in the dark: —She's very drunk—.

Swallowing hard, Yutaka whispered back: —Has Natchan been drinking?—

—Like a hippopotamus by the sound of it—.

—Is it safe for a woman to drink that much?—

— . . . Your Mom was always drinking. And then she went away and left you—.

Yutaka could find nothing to say to that, so he closed his eyes and tried to picture the mother he could only distantly recall. Her face and her voice were obscured by his aunt's, however, and he hadn't a hope of pinning down the elusive outlines that were hers alone. He suspected he might actually come closer to his impression of his mother if he thought of the cat belonging to the house behind theirs. She often slipped through a gap in the wooden fence to sprawl in the shade in their overgrown yard. She was so big and fat that from indoors she might have been taken for a bulldog. She always slept contentedly, but if Yutaka so much as set foot over the edge of the veranda she would spring up, bristle and glare at him with golden eyes, and dart away like a flying squirrel.

While he was pursuing the fleeing she-cat's shape Yutaka had dropped off to sleep. When he woke in the morning his aunt was fixing breakfast with her usual cross expression and Yutaka had all but forgotten her drunken homecoming of the night before.

As his grandfather's words came back to mind after lunch, Yutaka suddenly felt strangled by giant invisible hands. Did the fact that she'd been drinking mean she was about to go away? Did it mean that his aunt would disappear without trace like his mother, who'd run away time after time till she'd finally abandoned him? But in that case how could his grandfather remain so calm? Did he have some grounds for reassurance that Yutaka hadn't heard yet? That faraway look didn't give much cause for confidence. Perhaps his grandfather was just pretending not to know what was going on because he was

5

chicken. Though Yutaka wouldn't have dared ask his aunt a direct question either, of course. With each passing minute his mouth grew drier and his body so rusty that if he moved a finger the creaking sound threatened to reverberate around the room.

Seizing his chance while his aunt was in the toilet and the washing machine was running, Yutaka scuttled over to his grandfather and whispered in his ear: —Why haven't you asked Natchan? Maybe she's forgotten to go to the pool—.

His grandfather answered sourly: —You'll soon see. I'll get it out of her in a casual sort of way. You'd better keep quiet, now, Yutaka. One word about pools or sweethearts and there's no telling what'll happen.—

—Why?—

—Natchan doesn't want us to find out—.

True, they'd never heard her say in so many words that she was going to the pool. Since she hung her bathing suit out on the line she could hardly imagine she was keeping it from them entirely, but perhaps she did think of it as her secret.

Yutaka's aunt had never let him into her room. Whenever curiosity drove him to peek inside, she'd slap his cheek, sending Yutaka wailing to his grandfather. In another week or so, wanting something to eat he'd go looking for his aunt in her room, and when he found her there she'd twist his arm. Again he'd run screaming to his grandfather. By the time he started kindergarten, these repeated scenes had convinced Yutaka that his aunt was protecting her room so as not to be mistaken for his mother. Admittedly until he was four or five Yutaka had often forgotten and called her 'Mommy'. He was six or seven when he learned to catch an accidental 'Mo – ' just in time to correct himself to 'Natchan'. Nowadays he never made that mistake, not even in his dreams. At the same time, he'd learned the knack of approaching his aunt.

Though always sullen and cross, his aunt was not a bitter person at heart. Grandfather often murmured sadly, 'Natchan's what you might call her own worst enemy. Really she's a sweet girl who loves company.' One day Yutaka's mother had turned up very pregnant; she had shut herself away at home for three years and then quite suddenly ran off leaving the child behind. It was then that his aunt had

6

reluctantly given up her job at a kindergarten to become private nurse-maid to Yutaka and his grandfather, but perhaps what had worked at the kindergarten didn't work at home, for she had soon dropped the cheerful expression she used to wear for the children and became nervy and silent instead. Of course, this too was his grandfather's account, and Yutaka sympathised with his aunt without having a very good grasp of his own circumstances. (As a matter of fact the knowledge that a grown-up was making a sacrifice for his sake and no one else's aroused more satisfaction than sympathy; he didn't see anything wrong with a motherless child like himself having at least an aunt to tie down.) One little boy so weak he could be bullied by the girls in his class, and one invalid grandfather who could barely make it to the bathroom: naturally somebody had to take care of them, just as somebody had to water the flowers in the pots.

—But things can be hard to accept even if you know them to be so—his grandfather would say pensively. —It's not that Natchan doesn't like you, Yutaka, it's just that she can't forgive your Mommy. Coming home when she pleased, taking off again when she pleased. Even then it might have been easier if we'd never heard from her again, but instead she sends a little money now and then, so Natchan doesn't know what to think, she doesn't know if she's just minding you or if she's to keep you till you're grown up. And your Mom never gives her address. Poor Natchan must sometimes want to strangle us both.—

Frightened, Yutaka sifted frantically through his memory and came up with his grandfather's own words: —But you said Natchan was solid. You said she was strong.—

—Oh, of course, anyone but Natchan would have lost all patience and cleared out long ago. We're lucky it was Natchan who stayed. Now if she'd just take up some sort of outside interest like a young girl should, she might begin to settle down. There's nothing like a bit of fun to take your mind off your troubles . . . —

Remembering these words when his aunt began seeing the man from the building site next door and then going regularly to the pool, Yutaka had readily accepted these things as her outside interests. If it would ease her mind he'd be happy to see her go out more, to all kinds of places with all kinds of people. During summer vacation he

7

could mind the house and take naps with his grandfather, and once school started what happened in the daytime would be no concern of his. (Also, if the truth be told, while his aunt was away Yutaka and his grandfather secretly enjoyed a taste of freedom.)

If only they could find out whether or not she was going to the pool, they could at least relax. In his impatience Yutaka came close to taking it up with his aunt several times, but in case she stormed out of the house for good at the mention of the word 'pool' when she mightn't even have been planning to go, he searched for an indirect approach. Failing to find one, he could only keep quiet and watch for clues. Despite his grandfather's assurance that he'd get it out of her, his courage seemed to have deserted him, for since then he'd been pretending to be asleep. His aunt, of course, said not a word. It was two hours past her usual departure time, and during those two hours all three had remained silent – even the TV was switched off. At a loose end, Yutaka had begun stacking blocks one by one while he pictured his aunt in her bathing suit, the profile of her sweetheart whom he'd seen on a number of occasions, and his aunt's rear view as she left the house for ever, a big rucksack on her back and a bundle in each hand; but meanwhile his thoughts had strayed from his real-life worries and been drawn to the sea, where some of his classmates had boasted their parents were taking them this summer. His idea of the sea recalled the ocean around a tiny atoll in an adventure series on TV the week before. Its surface glittered sharply, as if countless slivers of glass hung suspended . . .

'I can't hear anything.' His aunt, who had paused over the ironing and was looking absently at a couple of flies buzzing overhead, suddenly spoke irritably and gave the grandfather a hard look. He turned and smiled at her.

'Oh? . . . You can't hear it, Natchan? That splashing noise, as if there's someone swimming in the air or under the floor.'

'Splashing?'

The aunt's eyes, for one moment round as marbles, narrowed suspiciously. When it dawned on Yutaka that this was his grandfather's 'casual sort of way', he shrank involuntarily and observed his aunt's reaction with care. His grandfather, looking distinctly uncomfortable, went on telling lies.

'I wonder if something's wrong with my ears. It sounds exactly like splashing. In fact it sounds like the breaststroke . . . That reminds me, you used to be good at the breaststroke, didn't you, Natchan? It sounds as if there's another Natchan swimming on the roof . . . Yutaka, you hear it too, don't you?'

Yutaka answered timidly, 'Mm . . . a bit.' He sneaked a glance at his grandfather, who lay in bed with his cotton robe open at the chest. His grandfather gave an answering twitch of the right corner of his lips. Emboldened, Yutaka went on. 'But I thought it came from the kitchen. Whenever Natchan goes to the pool, you see, I always hear the same noise.'

His aunt had dropped her eyes and was putting away the iron. At her elbow teetered a pile of neatly folded shirts and blouses. Just a little more prompting and she'd answer. She'd let them catch a glimpse of what was on her mind, thought Yutaka, gaining courage from the convincing lie that had popped out of his mouth. His grandfather must have sensed the same thing; his voice, picking up Yutaka's cue, grew steadily louder.

'Now that you mention it, maybe I have heard it before. I guess it only bothered me today because Natchan's here. But it's strange that she can't hear it.'

' . . . That is strange, isn't it?'

' . . . She's usually having a swim at this time of day, isn't she? Maybe since she isn't there today the pool has come to call her.'

The aunt, her face still lowered, started sorting the pressed clothes into piles for each member of the family. They'd have their answer any moment now. Tensely, Yutaka gripped the blocks on his knees. Natchan, his grandfather had once told him, was the type who followed orders, who went along with whoever invited her, and it seemed he'd been right. That remark was probably made when his aunt first began visiting the building site next door.

— . . . What I'm saying is that there are two kinds of people: those who use and those who are used. The users unconsciously attract the usable type and then get what they want with the greatest of ease. Those who are used may not like it, but before they know what's happening they're trying to show that no one could be more devoted than they are. It seems people are born as one type or the other. Natchan will be used until the day she dies, and there's not a thing she can do to change it. I don't know who will use her, but someone will . . . Us? I wonder which type we are . . . —

Yutaka saw his aunt about to walk away with the iron in her hand and before he could stop himself cried chokingly, 'Natchan!'

His grandfather's voice called her name at the same instant: 'Natchan, where are you going?'

Brought to a halt by this duet, she stood stock-still and reddening like a pupil ordered to her feet in class, turned to them and burst out, 'What are you two after, wheedling like a couple of spoiled kids?' She fled to her room. In his disappointment Yutaka hurled the block in his hand at the TV. They daren't upset his aunt or they couldn't even count on dinner. At the thought of spending a second night with an empty stomach a shiver ran through him. And after they'd been so concerned and so patient. It wasn't fair. Yutaka imagined himself as a detective extracting the criminal's confession: he would sit astride his aunt's body pulling her hair and banging her forehead on the floor till he forced her to answer his questions one by one.

For a start he'd have to ask whether she was ever going to the pool again. Come on, out with it! Between birdlike cries as he hurt her head, she would answer that she'd given up going to the pool. Pressing his advantage he'd demand to know why. For a moment his aunt would struggle violently under him. He'd give her hair a good yank and dig his feet into her sides. Weeping, she would confess haltingly that she'd quarrelled last night with her sweetheart. Yutaka would carry on the interrogation in a low, controlled voice, swinging her head mercilessly from side to side. Why did you quarrel? It's no good trying to hide anything from me. Tell the truth or I'll have your scalp. His aunt would wet her pants from pain and fear, and her crying would turn high and thin. Last night, my sweetheart, he tried to look at me where it's rude. Did he only try to look? Yutaka demands. He didn't touch you? A bit. And what did you do? Answer! Quick! The aunt replies faintly: I didn't say anything. I ran. He was going to molest you, wasn't he? Yutaka grills his aunt. I knew it all along. Didn't you? His aunt's whole body trembles. She is trying to speak but her voice doesn't reach Yutaka's ears. Crying

10

won't help. I've no sympathy for you. You've only yourself to blame. What did you see in him? His aunt weakly shakes her head. You were taken in by your sweetheart because you're a fool. From now on you're to think only of Grandpa and me. His aunt gives a barely perceptible nod. Answer me properly! She manages a shaky 'Yes'. Right, then, first you're taking me to the beach. You needn't take Grandpa. You hear me? . . .

Suddenly aware of his grandfather's eyes upon him, Yutaka heaved an exaggerated sigh and hid his blushes. Then he whispered gravely, 'Did I really sound spoiled?'

His grandfather smiled wryly and closed his eyes before replying. 'Not a bit . . . But I'm afraid we failed.'

'Looks like she's been *jilted* . . . don't you think?'

There was no answer.

Yutaka lay down beside his grandfather and traced his aunt's sweetheart's face in the air. According to his grandfather, the man from the building site was his aunt's first sweetheart. It's not uncommon when there are two sisters in the family, he'd added: the more outrageously and selfishly one behaves, the more circumspect the other becomes. Yutaka's mother and aunt were no exception. His aunt had always scorned such things as romantic novels and love letters, and after Yutaka's mother came home pregnant she'd turned more strait-laced and moralistic than ever till she eventually came to resemble Yutaka's grandmother, who all her life had smugly found fault with other people. That explained why Natchan had reached the age of twenty-six without having had a special boyfriend. Or at least (his grandfather conceded) not as far as he knew. If this time was the first, Yutaka wondered if that made it his aunt's *first love*.

Her *first love* had small slanting eyes, a large nose always florid with a number of pimples, and a heavy furrowed forehead the weight of which seemed to tip his face permanently forward, since Yutaka had never seen him look straight ahead. The man was so big that the aunt – a tall woman – had to tilt her head to talk to him, so for most purposes he probably never needed to look any higher than his eye level. In the black shirt he always wore, from a distance he resembled a dusty bear at the zoo. He could be seen standing aside and watching the other labourers hard at it, his expression implying that work didn't agree with him.

11

Yutaka had no idea how his aunt had become acquainted with the man. All he knew was that after the bulldozers entered the vacant site she took to gazing with interest from the veranda, since the machines were only partially visible from the kitchen window. Having heard his grandfather grumble a good deal on the subject, Yutaka assumed she was checking to see that the construction crew next door weren't up to anything for which they didn't have permission.

— . . . Up to a point it couldn't be helped, I suppose, but what's the good of our having meekly accepted what they offered? Now we'll have no say at all, they can put up any kind of building they like. Surely Natchan must've realised they were taking advantage of her? Ours is the only house that will get no sun. And they must've had a pretty good idea who lives here. That's why they brought cakes and goodies to steal a girl's heart. If only she'd made them talk to me, but no, the girl has to go and handle it herself. I'll bet they thought ho-ho, we've got them where we want them! Now if I was in good health I wouldn't let the matter rest till they paid compensation. They say three storeys, but who knows? What if they get above themselves and put up ten? I didn't keep the house all these years just to end up living under the eyes of who knows what sort of crowd. You watch: if a tall building goes up next door this'll rot around our ears. Didn't Natchan care what became of the old place? . . . What a blow. Never in my wildest dreams did I think we'd have an apartment block next door . . . — Yutaka had often heard this sad refrain, but the old man hid his dissatisfaction from the aunt herself and only asked from time to time how the work was progressing.

His grandfather's gloom, deep as it might be, couldn't make it rain on the construction site, and the builders with their battery of bulldozers and excavators made steady progress. The noise of earthmoving equipment shook Yutaka's house from morning to night. The wall clock went wrong, dishes spilled from kitchen shelves. Yutaka's grandfather moaned that they might as well be having daily earthquakes, and his temperature rose above normal. Yutaka, however, felt the vibrations each day in his own way. To him it seemed they had rapidly dissolved the opaque jelly that smothered the house, turning it to a hot, rushing stream. And from where the jelly had melted came light airy sounds he didn't recognise and yet somehow found familiar.

12

Sounds like cars swishing by, unseen people talking, footsteps; then again, they could be machines of all sizes heard from all directions.

Once the dissolving had started it wasn't humanly possible to stop it. The construction work next door had been sent down like the thunder or a blast of wind; to protest against it as his grandfather was doing seemed to Yutaka utter foolishness. At the same time he noticed that his house – which he'd believed till then to be the most comfortable and unchanging place in the world – was terribly small and old, and before long he was half hoping that the stream would knock it down. They gouged away the earth, poured in gravel and cement, drove piles. The huge machines next door hummed agreeably in Yutaka's ears. Watching from his favourite spot he'd mutter: Shake harder! Roar louder! For the first time Yutaka was excited to arrive home from school. What changes would he find? He'd have a good look at the site first, then glance over at his own house and be disappointed to see not a single tile dislodged. The concrete wall along the boundary huddled away from the hot flood in cowardly fashion and never displayed so much as a crack.

But the same lightness of heart that Yutaka felt showed up after a while in his aunt's expression. By that time the foundations were finished, steel uprights rose like the bars of a bird-cage, and Yutaka's excitement was beginning to subside.

At first he thought the change might be due to the season. It was mid-April, the time of year when Yutaka learned the 'Carp Streamers Song' at school. Even his ever-complaining grandfather was enjoying an occasional stroll in the yard, leaning on Yutaka. He would murmur dreamily, 'Smell those new leaves', 'Looks like the rambling rose will bloom for us this year', but sooner or later he always looked up at the steel posts next door as if seeing them for the first time and, after an emphatic tut-tut and a long sigh, fell silent. Meanwhile Yutaka's aunt seemed to have grown lighter in her spring clothes – even her hair seemed light. Avoiding Yutaka and his grandfather as much as possible, she began practising singing in her room and doing exercises on the veranda. In short, she acted like a child. Yutaka had to admit his aunt was conspicuously younger than his classmates' mothers – a fact he found more disturbing than pleasing. The person who brought him up ought to be a grown-up. Being a child himself,

Yutaka knew just how carefree and irresponsible children were. And sure enough, since this change had come over his aunt their dinners had deteriorated.

Yutaka was to discover the connection between his aunt's changed manner and the apartment block at about the time the steel supports, having been partitioned off into three levels, were being encased in concrete. As the aunt's new habit of going shopping from noon to two every day struck his grandfather as suspicious he got Yutaka to follow her. It wasn't natural, suddenly going to the market in the heat of the day, nor was it natural to come back with only a large radish and a couple of bean curd squares to show for two hours' shopping. Yutaka was of course delighted to undertake the mission – he very rarely got to go on a genuine tracking expedition.

But the expedition for which he'd so carefully prepared – even wearing the white running shoes he'd used on sports day – came to an abrupt end after a mere ten yards. No sooner had his aunt left the house with her shopping basket on her arm than she paused by the board fence two doors down and took a quick, nervous glance back. Yutaka barely managed to take cover behind a parked truck outside the site, and at that same moment grey overalls brushed past his head. When he tentatively poked it round the corner again after catching his breath, his aunt was entering the grounds of the little temple across the road, and at her side was a strange man from the construction site. The area was a favourite playground for local children – Yutaka had sometimes gone there shyly himself – but none of them would be there in the middle of the day. Suddenly losing his nerve, Yutaka ran trembling back to the house to report what he'd seen. His grandfather simply nodded and murmured, 'So that's it.'

After that, Yutaka saw his aunt many times sitting beside the big man on the graveyard fence. Sometimes they were munching sandwiches out of a shared bag; sometimes they were smoking. And once the big man was crouched with his face buried between the aunt's breasts while she uneasily twirled his hair.

Yutaka and his grandfather were afraid of what his aunt might do when the apartment block was finished. When the big man was gone she'd take it out on them more spitefully than ever. Worse still, she might leave home after him. Hearing his grandfather worry aloud

14

about the possibility and feeling compelled to do something, Yutaka proposed eagerly that they have the man to live with them in the spare room. Apparently that wouldn't work, however. The aunt didn't want them to see her sweetheart. Remember how she'd let fly at Yutaka when she caught him spying? His grandfather's words brought back sharply a scene from several weeks ago.

He was up a tree watching the big man at work when his aunt rushed over with the clothes-pole and began prodding his bottom and hissing, 'Get down, silly, you'll fall.' Yutaka clung to the trunk.

'No,' he insisted, 'I want to watch the workmen.'

'What's so special about an old building site? They're everywhere.'

On a wicked impulse Yutaka said very loudly, 'Natchan, I bet you'd like to watch, really, wouldn't you?'

His aunt's face flushed visibly, and a moment later the clothes-pole gave Yutaka's rear a vigorous prod. Yutaka screamed and hugged the trunk for dear life.

'You sneak, Natchan!'

'If you're so keen to watch, you can stay up there till it gets dark. Don't you know how Grandpa hates the building?'

'I know, I know! Stop, I won't watch any more!'

In terror of being knocked to the ground, he'd given in despite himself; then he realised that his aunt had cleverly switched the reason for her anger, and he took a closer look at her face. She scowled up at him, wielding the pole furiously, her brows puckered, cheeks hollow, almost in tears. Would it be so dreadful if he found out about her sweetheart? Yutaka was puzzled.

The apartment block was completed at the beginning of July, shortly before Yutaka's school was to be let out for the summer. The workers' prefab quarters were hauled away, the tiles were polished on the outer walls, and flowers were planted beside the entrance. It wasn't long before peace was restored next door and his aunt was her old self again. But no, there was something different about her: from behind she seemed hunched as if with age, and her sarcastic remarks grew more frequent. She could often be seen squatting in the kitchen staring tirelessly at the vegetable rack and its jumble of onions and radishes; at such times she was deaf to Yutaka no matter how loud he yelled. His grandfather, having feared the worst, didn't know what to make of this. 'Do you suppose they were only eating lunch together after all?' he asked, to which Yutaka replied with all the wisdom he could command:

'If you ask me, Natchan liked the building site more than she liked that man. So now the building's finished she doesn't need him any more.'

His grandfather nodded as if he saw the sense of this. Yet their expressions continued to warn each other that it couldn't be true, that something bad had to happen any day.

Soon, they began to see movers outside the neighbouring apartments. Whenever Yutaka detected the sound of a van pulling up he'd race outside, through the yard to the gate, and from there he'd secretly greet the newcomers. One Sunday vans arrived four times. They were all identical, and the families who rode in them were all alike too. They had pale, exhausted faces. Under their direction the loads of furniture were carried in with such care they might have been coffins. Couches, TVs, refrigerators, washing machines, chests of drawers, tables, all were transported compliantly into the building's white lobby.

While Yutaka was occupied with the moving in, his aunt had begun her trips to the pool.

When would Natchan settle down? Wasn't Grandpa taking things too casually? . . . Yutaka impatiently studied the dozing old man's features there beside him. No wonder Mommy ran out on us. How on earth does he plan to live if Natchan disappears? We'll starve to death, and what's more in this heat we'll rot like the watermelon rinds that the garbage trucks drop by the roadside. His grandfather had told him about tatami mats rotting, but they'd rot faster themselves. Yutaka scrambled to his feet thinking he'd caught a whiff of decay. He looked down at his grandfather's face, stiff and yellow in sleep, and clenched his fist. They wouldn't catch him dying there with the old coot.

Just then his aunt slipped from her room, having changed into a sky-blue cotton shirt and jeans. Coming face to face with Yutaka who froze and stared, she forced a smile and, quickly averting her eyes, crossed to the kitchen sink. After drinking down a glass of water, she

16

checked her watch and murmured to no one in particular, 'I'm really very late.'

Yutaka gaped at his aunt. Her face was flushed and swollen. The end of her nose was especially bright. Wherever she was headed, he knew at once she mustn't be allowed to go now. But no words came. Yutaka followed with extreme caution, stepping as if his ankles were roped together, as she went into the hall. She was carrying the white basket she'd taken with her every day. But her bathing suit couldn't be in there. Her bathing suit was still hanging on the line. She must have accidentally left it behind. For a second he thought of running to fetch it and flinging it at her, but he couldn't guarantee she'd still be there. He had to speak out – clearly, so clearly that Natchan would squeeze his hand and burst into tears of repentance for the way she'd acted till now. Keeping his eyes glued to his aunt stooping to buckle her sandals, Yutaka made several attempts to speak, stopped, and swallowed hard.

As his aunt straightened and reached for the door Yutaka made up his mind. His voice came out more cracked than his grandfather's. But he couldn't do anything about that now.

'Take care. Don't catch cold . . . '

His aunt's body rocked as if jolted in the back, but immediately she drew herself up and turned her head. Yutaka struggled to smile and nod, his face looking all the while as if he were about to sneeze.

Saying nothing, his aunt knitted her brows and began to inspect Yutaka slowly from head to foot. He in turn sneaked a look at her small bust, her neck and its two moles, her legs in their loose blue jeans, and her face, level with his as she stood below the hall step. The face was a glossy red and the cluster of pimples around her mouth more prominent than usual, making him think of an over-ripe strawberry. He had to remind her quickly about the bathing suit. He was annoyed with himself for losing his nerve, he fought to stop himself running away, but as long as his aunt's eyes were on him he couldn't shape his lips into anything but that smile.

I guess Natchan *would* want to leave us – I wouldn't want to be landed with such a little sissy kid myself. Go, then! . . . Growing confused under his aunt's grimly held stare, Yutaka had begun to cry while still smiling.

He raised his eyes to the ceiling, determined that no stupid tears

17

should fall. As one did trickle onto his cheek, however, his aunt stretched out her left hand and gave his ear lobe a tug. Then she stuck out her chin and sniggered. But she regained her solemnity at once, said quietly, 'Mind your own business . . . Sissy. What you need is a little brother,' then ducked through the door and ran off.

Left behind, Yutaka sat down on the cold concrete of the porch floor, rubbed his face in both hands, and set about analysing this behaviour of his aunt's while studying the lint accumulated along the wall. Perhaps crying had been the right thing to do. She'd pulled his ear: had that meant 'Why are you crying when you know I'll come home?' Or did she mean 'If you must cry, cry like a man'? Either way, his aunt hadn't been able to ignore Yutaka's tears. So even if she had been planning to leave, clearly she'd put it off for today, otherwise she wouldn't have said what she did on the way out. She was pleased by Yutaka's concern, that's why she said it. And when people are leaving for good – this was the clincher – they don't say anything. Remembering his mother, Yutaka was somewhat reassured. Maybe he'd been worrying himself altogether too much. His aunt might be his mother's sister, but they were complete opposites. It was his mother who'd been in the habit of running off, not his aunt.

His mother had run away four times, counting successes and failures, starting at nineteen. Each time, so he'd been told, she disappeared without a word before anybody caught on. She did have a reason the first time – she refused to stick around to be the household cook, she was going to put herself through photography school and become a top photographer – but later on she left for no apparent cause, simply out of habit, just as Yutaka's grandfather liked to gargle after meals. Running away out of habit was more of a problem than the other kind, since there was no way to stop it. The family was sure she'd have learned her lesson after Yutaka was born, yet in the third year the habit came back and away she went. So suddenly that Grandpa thought at first she'd been kidnapped. And Yutaka remembered nothing of what had happened. He couldn't imagine himself chasing after her, crying. But it seems he'd spent ten whole days going into the porch and crying his eyes out. All he could remember was the voices of his aunt and grandfather raised in argument afterwards. His aunt sobbed as if her own mother had vanished. His grandfather stroked his face and groaned. Yutaka remembered his surprise as he watched and realised: his mother wasn't his alone.

At the time his aunt had accused him: —Why didn't you stop her? You were with her, weren't you?—

—I dunno . . . —

—How stupid can you get? You and Grandpa were both there, and you didn't notice a thing! So you saw her off without a peep, did you, Yutaka? With your mouth hanging open?—

—I dunno . . . —

When Yutaka returned to their shared room, his grandfather wasn't asleep but propped on his elbow, engrossed in television. Yutaka sat on the veranda and, having first checked that the white bathing suit was still on the line, had a look at the fuzzy screen. A man was slicing a radish and talking politely. Yutaka was vaguely reminded of his aunt's sweetheart.

'Has she gone?' his grandfather asked, not taking his eyes off the TV.

'Mm . . . When did you wake up, Grandpa?'

'I was never asleep. I knew she'd go out if I dropped off . . . So, did she say anything?'

'Mm. "Mind your own business" . . . '

Finding it strangely bothersome to answer his grandfather, Yutaka wasted no words.

'What'd she mean by that?'

'I don't know . . . What's he making?'

His grandfather continued his own questions: 'Was that all she said?'

'Mm . . . After that, she said I ought to have a little brother.' As he spoke Yutaka raised his eyes to the roof of the apartment building and caught sight of two children capering there, naked. From where he sat he had only the briefest of glimpses, but they seemed to be having fun with water, for mixed with the toddlers' squeals was the sound of splashing.

'Did she mean . . . she'd make one for you? Why did she come out with a thing like that? Hey, Yutaka?'

His grandfather's voice grew steadily louder. Not heeding the question Yutaka went barefoot into the yard for a better look at the children on the roof. Though only a short distance separated him from them, their voices carried like a remote mountain echo. His grandfather's voice from the house was three times as loud. Between the two sounds, Yutaka tried hard to remember how the foundation work had sounded in the spring.

'. . . I don't believe Natchan would do anything so drastic. And there's no guaranteeing she could look after you *and* her own child without favouritism. Natchan doesn't know your father. This couldn't possibly solve anything unless she didn't know either of the fathers. Her ideas have certainly taken a peculiar turn. There's her sister's example, I suppose, but after all the harsh things she's said about her – what can she be thinking of? Or – could it be on the way already? . . . '

'Silly old windbag,' Yutaka said to himself and smiled with his back to his grandfather. Then he shrilled the command and swung into the warming-up exercises he'd been taught in swimming class. The voices on the apartment roof continued to echo like the cries of birds swooping over the sea. Above the voices, the splashing reached his ears with increasing force. Through it he detected the pleasant hum of the construction work.

Yutaka had never shown such spirit doing the exercises at school.

One-two-three, one-two-three . . . Now then, shall we make a start? Don't forget to wet your body first, or you can have a heart attack – in other words, you'll die. If you don't want to die, make sure you wet yourself down first. Good, now we're ready for the sea. Follow me and take it easy. Don't rush. There's plenty of time. Sea bathing should be taken nice and easy. If you rush in it's dangerous. Tread carefully. One step at a time. Here comes a wave – now don't be scared, stand still and wait, take it with your chest. Natchan! You're facing the wrong way! You'll fall over . . . Now what did I tell you? No use crying, it's your own fault. Did you get a mouthful? Why didn't you listen to me? The waves can be dangerous if you let them scare you. Don't cry – you're a big girl of five, aren't you? And you, my girl, what are you laughing at? That's not very nice, is it? Rub your little sister's back. No? Hey! You push her head under like that and by golly, she'll drown! Hold it, here's another wave. Don't cry, Natchan, or you'll get another mouthful . . . All right, you two? Fine.

20

Then why are you crying, Natchan? I can't stand children who blubber. My goodness, where's your sister off to? Don't you go off like that. Wait! I said wait! Natchan, stop that crying! And where's your sister? – you come back here this minute. The sea's no place to play tag . . .

Yutaka had slipped himself into a scene from one of his grandfather's reminiscences.

S O U T H · W I N D

'I may have an opportunity to visit your area in the spring. It would give me great pleasure if, while there, I could satisfy myself that you are well . . . '

That winter Akiko had received a postcard with this message from Toyokichi Satō.

Why in the spring? It struck Akiko as a little odd. The Toyokichi she remembered wasn't a man to fear the cold, despite his age. And if he had it in mind to reassure himself that Akiko was all right, she would have thought he'd seek her out with all speed and not let a thing like the season or the weather make a day's difference.

Akiko couldn't forget the figure of old man Toyokichi, a large sketchbook under his arm, striding lightly up a steep mountain road against the wind. He'd overtaken her on the road, though she'd had a head start, and put distance between them in the twinkling of an eye. Only the wind, gusting hard enough to bring down trees, remained behind with her. She'd been struggling up the road, daunted by the wind, and was left feeling more alone than before.

This business of 'in the spring' was out of character. Bothered by the roundabout wording, she'd been on the point of replying, 'Don't worry, I'm alive all right.' But her correspondent was an old man with time on his hands. No need to take him seriously, Akiko told herself, it was just one of his jottings on the spur of the moment. Beginning to feel increasingly irked by the leisurely old man, she had stuck the card in a drawer and never read it again. At the time Kawamura's wife had just died, the baby was crawling and needed to be watched constantly, and night after night she would mutter to herself in bed, 'But I can't go on like this. I've got to start work.'

Then she was off, taking the baby on her back and visiting a friend who was in insurance, following up her introductions to insurance companies, making repeated trips to the welfare office to enroll the baby in a nursery, and all the while keeping up a running argument with Kawamura when he occasionally came over – till before she knew it spring had arrived. The magnolia next door to her apartment was in flower again this year, and on the first day at the nursery the one cherry tree growing in its small garden was scattering petals.

Hearing at her back the cries of the baby in an attendant's arms, Akiko began work that day for an insurance company. After six months she would be placed on the permanent payroll. She repeated to herself what her friend had said: 'People make fun of canvassing, but it's really a first-rate job.' The friend now earned close to two hundred thousand yen a month. The mere thought of such an income gave her a thrill of anticipation that almost took her breath away. Gone were the days of those demeaning labels – 'Kawamura's mistress', 'illegitimate child' – when all he gave her was eighty thousand in support. Her cheeks aglow, Akiko couldn't help picturing a reunion with her daughter, now ten years old, whom she had left with her ex-husband.

The daily round was hectic where before it had been anything but: rush to the nursery in the morning with the baby on her back, rush on to the office, pound the streets of the district through the day, rush back to the nursery in the evening, pick up a bagful of dirty diapers, bibs, and towels and strap the baby on her back, shop on the way home, and once there – not stopping to sit down – prepare the baby's food, do the washing, heat a bath. When she'd put the baby to bed, drowsiness would lure her as she folded diapers and watched TV, and there were nights when she would drop off in front of the set.

Kawamura, who lived with his elderly mother and teenage daughter, would not allow himself to stay at Akiko's after his wife died. As long as she wasn't working he would find time now and then to call in during the day, but once that became impossible he looked in at night and returned home in the small hours. He would try to catch her in his arms as if there wasn't a moment to spare, insisting this was his apartment, his child, his woman, as Akiko gritted her teeth and hit, scratched, and kicked, but she was no match for Kawamura's strength and would be under his body in no time. The first contact of his skin's warmth touched off a nostalgia for his desire, as for a thing of the distant past. If she was going to have to anyway, why not? And she would want to give his desire release.

Listening to him slip out of bed, dress quietly, open the door, and leave, Akiko would realise that once again she had let Kawamura get away with it, and she would grind her teeth in frustration at her own complicity. A shameful ambivalence no longer allowed her to blame only the man.

Often, on getting up the next morning, she would have bruises on her arms and legs.

The baby didn't take well to the nursery and began to cry in the night, perhaps with bad dreams, and was slow to stop even when cuddled or given a bottle. In the mornings, too, the crying accompanied her out of the nursery, and as she walked along a street in the middle of the day she would feel as though she were hauling a dragnet of the baby's cries around her hips. A long, transparent net: when she looked back there would be the sea in the distance, her net vanishing into its blue surface and the baby's cries hovering in its waters like a school of silver sardines.

One day in particular, a light rain had fallen since morning – a soundless, glistening rain.

That day Akiko received another postcard from old man Toyokichi. 'I've developed kidney trouble,' it said, 'and have been in the hospital since March. I'm afraid this is no time for a sketching trip, but considering my age I've half resigned myself. Since you're still young I expect you're keeping as busy as ever, but I'm concerned at not having heard from you. I do hope nothing is wrong.' With the baby in its sling on her back, Akiko read and reread the message. She was surprised at her extreme disappointment. Tears came into her eyes as she thought: Oh, he can't come. Spring's here and I won't be seeing him. It was the first time she'd realised how impatiently she was awaiting old man Toyokichi's visit.

Akiko had received an annual New Year's card from old man Toyokichi. While regarding it as something of a chore, she had sent him one in return each year. Because she waited to write until she'd seen the old man's card, she posted her reply each time on the third of January. That was the extent of their friendship, which had lasted six years. This year, too, one of the seven cards in the special New Year's day delivery had been from Toyokichi.

The cards that came for Akiko dwindled steadily year by year, and there'd been one fewer again this January. The one that didn't come was from her ex-husband's younger sister, with whom she had remained friendly. Her mother, her older brother, a niece who was at high school, her younger sister, a friend from the housing estate where she'd lived with her husband, her friend at the insurance company, and Toyokichi Satō. The old man's card was important to Akiko for the sake of numbers, but as she gazed at the seven cards she'd made up her mind that if there was going to be one fewer next year, this was the one to cut out. The trouble with you, she told herself, is that you keep on idly humouring this elderly gentleman. Everything had changed completely in the past six years, but the old man was incapable of accepting change. Old Toyokichi still believed that Akiko's daughter was with her. He took it for granted that she was enjoying the occasional sketching trip while she brought up her daughter as usual.

Old Toyokichi's New Year's cards varied so little from year to year that it was tempting to think even the wording in the small feminine hand was the same. She couldn't compare them as she made a habit of throwing out those that didn't win a prize in the post office's New Year's lottery. But she was sure the last one had also read: 'How have you been? I expect your daughter has grown. Do you still draw? I keep active with my sketching trips.' In short, Akiko thought, she also represented just so much, and no more, to Toyokichi.

Toyokichi himself probably had hardly anyone to send his New Year's greetings to. He probably wanted to make sure of receiving every one he could get. She could guess the situation at home, where the family would pay little attention to what they considered his eccentric ways; for that very reason she hadn't been able to turn her back on him sooner, but she was in no position now to be keeping the old man company. It was time to leave behind the Akiko to whom the old man had taken a liking, the Akiko who felt a sympathy with the old man.

Kawamura's wife had been in a coma then. He and his daughter had begun taking turns sleeping in the hospital room, and even when seeing Akiko he talked of nothing but his wife's condition. Not that she didn't understand his anxiety – it was serious, without question. But she couldn't feel anything like the concern that Kawamura did, and his incessant talk of his wife's snore, her colouring, the number of injections she was having, and so forth, exasperated her beyond bearing.

For the first time, Akiko had not replied to old man Toyokichi. And at the end of January a postcard had arrived from him with a hasty note: 'I didn't receive a card from you this New Year. Whatever can be the matter? I trust all is well.' Akiko was baffled – what was he so worried about? While she was at a loss for a reply Kawamura's wife had indeed passed away, and until his second inquiry arrived she had entirely forgotten about old man Toyokichi's solicitude.

The day Toyokichi's third postcard came was a Saturday. Getting home in the rain with a week's bundle of used sheets and bath towels from the nursery in addition to the usual bag of diapers, and perspiring under the weight of the baby on her back, she made the rare discovery of a postcard in her box.

She read it on the spot, beside the tiers of mailboxes in the foyer, and again after reaching her fourth-floor apartment and shedding her load, and again while running the washing machine. As she changed the baby, who had woken from a nap, she put the postcard down where she could see it out of the corner of her eye. She had a feeling that the writing was bigger than usual – perhaps he'd written it lying in bed? She hung the washing to dry indoors and began the week's cleaning. The baby played tirelessly in the kitchen, rolling the pots and kettle about.

She put together a simple evening meal from what she had on hand, fed the baby and hurried through her own meal before the baby could interrupt, then sprawled on the tatami after dumping the dirty dishes in the sink and carefully inspected the card once more. He had used a black felt-tip pen. She was sure it had been a ball point before. No doubt one didn't get a free choice of writing materials in a hospital. She enjoyed deciphering the illegible postmark as if it were a puzzle, and pictured various kinds of hospital from the name he had given in his address. It didn't sound like a private hospital, nor a large general hospital. It was in a rapidly growing dormitory town in the next prefecture which was also, she knew, the town where old man Toyokichi lived. Though she had often heard of it, Akiko had never been there.

That night Kawamura came while it was still early. The baby, who had recently become shy with strangers, took one look and burst into tears. 'Why the hell don't you teach the kid to know his father?' Kawamura said sharply.

Akiko didn't retort as she might once have done, 'I will when you recognise him as yours.' Not even turning toward Kawamura, she took the baby on her knee and pressed her cheek to his head. The baby's head was hot. She did intend, certainly, to teach him that Kawamura was his father, but she would not let him think he should be dependent on the man. Since Kawamura's wife had died Akiko herself had been wanting to slip quickly out of Kawamura's domain. She could no longer understand why she'd been so preoccupied with little things like paternity and divorce. She was the mother of two children. The mother of a ten-year-old daughter and an eight-month-old son. Kawamura had his domain, and she had hers.

At the thought that if it hadn't been for his wife's death she would herself have been hanging on Kawamura's arm in the same blind way, Akiko couldn't help being grateful for the unexpected turn that events had taken. Regretful, also: if only she'd come to her senses while Kawamura's wife was still alive, she could have let her die more peacefully. Kawamura, suffering the same remorse, was irritable with Akiko, and increasingly tenacious.

Akiko had once accidentally run into Kawamura out for a walk with his teenage daughter. It was towards the close of the previous year, when Kawamura's wife was already in the hospital. Akiko had the baby out in the stroller and was feeding breadcrumbs to the pigeons that flocked in the square outside the railway station. This was something she had taken to doing while expecting the baby. Sitting on a bench, sunning herself as she followed the pigeons' movements, she would be enveloped in a sense of well-being that captured for her what the word *happiness* meant. There were others who passed the time daydreaming on the same bench – an old man with an infant, a youth

27

who seemed to live alone. But though they knew each other by sight, they would casually turn their faces away.

Had Kawamura and his daughter – an only child – been taking a train to visit Kawamura's wife? The pigeons pecking at crumbs around Akiko's feet suddenly all flew up at once, and the wind and whirr of their wings made the baby laugh out loud. This brought a smile to Akiko's lips; at the same moment she noticed the figures of a girl and her father standing to her left before the station kiosk, looking up at the flock of pigeons wheeling in the sky. The plump girl wore a white overcoat.

Perhaps Kawamura sensed Akiko observing him, for his head turned quickly in their direction. Holding the baby's hand, Akiko watched Kawamura with her mouth open. Kawamura also parted his lips, but his expression was fixed. Then, urging along his daughter, who was still gazing into the sky, he hurried off toward the ticket gate.

The girl hadn't been told, even now, of the existence of her eight-month-old brother. Kawamura intended to conceal his affair with Akiko until his aged mother died and his daughter married, and he couldn't forgive Akiko for openly enrolling the baby in a public nursery centre run by the local council.

'What's this?' Kawamura muttered as his eye fell on Toyokichi's postcard lying on the table. When she realised what he was referring to, Akiko burst out so loudly that she gave herself a start, 'Don't touch that!' And only when she had snatched the card from his hand, shut it in the drawer, and turned the key could she breathe easily and murmur, loud enough for Kawamura to hear, 'Phew, that was close.'

'What the . . . ?' Kawamura forced a smile.

' . . . My pen pal,' Akiko replied, also with a smile.

'Pen pal?' Kawamura repeated blankly, then laughed, his mouth wide open. Akiko was tickled too, and as she laughed the baby on her lap looked up at its mother's face and put its hand in her mouth.

'Hello there.' Akiko picked up the baby and handed it to Kawamura. This time it didn't cry.

'Come on, put your hand in my mouth too.' Kawamura opened his mouth as far as it would go and presented it in front of the baby's face. The baby stiffened in fright and stared wide-eyed at the strange world inside. It had been a long time since Akiko laughed so hard that her sides ached.

That night, again, Kawamura went home without a word after midnight.

When she had heard the door close and the sound of his shoes fade in the distance, Akiko got up, took a look at the sleeping baby's face, and slid open the glass doors behind the curtains. The daylong rain had lifted at last. She stepped into sandals and went out onto the balcony. Perhaps the sky was still clouded, for she couldn't find the moon. The magnolias had long since dropped from the tree next door, which was fringed with yellow-green young leaves. As there were many private houses in the neighbourhood that hadn't yet been redeveloped, the view was quite extensive for a fourth-floor room. Lighted windows were dotted below, their gleams transforming the blue darkness to an expanse of ocean. The rain-dampened air heightened the sense of the sea.

Akiko tried to recall what she'd been like when she met old man Toyokichi six years earlier.

Her daughter was only four. What had prompted her to leave daughter and husband and go on a trip alone? She racked her memory. She didn't know Kawamura then, nor was she unhappy with her husband. Her daughter was growing into a fine healthy child, and life was going so smoothly that when Akiko's mother came to visit from the country she would counsel caution: this was all very well, but she shouldn't take her happiness for granted. Was that what, in the end, she had done?

She couldn't remember the circumstances at all, but she must have declared to her husband that she wanted some time off by herself, even just a night away, and set out in triumph. Akiko found it strange: why had she so little recollection of what must have been no small event for her? When she was at college and having trouble settling into the women's dormitory, she would often go travelling alone. She supposed that one day, four years after her daughter was born, the sensations of those solitary trips had suddenly come back to her and wouldn't be brushed away.

She went to the mountains, an hour and a half by special express from downtown Tokyo. Though close to the city, the village she'd picked was difficult of access with no bus service. According to her guidebook there were inns in the village which still used kerosene lamps, and this phrase had attracted her. It was late March, past the snow season, but at the end of the line the other passengers leaving the express were all local people. Consulting her map she found the route, a mountain road wide enough for cars, but even with no more luggage than a shoulder bag it wasn't an easy matter for Akiko to climb the steep slope directly into the strong wind that was, un-luckily, raging that day. From the station to her destination was two hours' journey. On the way she was overtaken by the old man with his rucksack and sketchbook. From his swift stride she took him for a local.

It was about two o'clock when she reached her goal. She had planned to enjoy the surrounding scenery before making her way to an inn, but, deterred by the wind, she took refuge in the first bed-and-breakfast that caught her eye. She opened the sliding glass doors to find old man Toyokichi sitting beside a sunken hearth in the earthen-floored hall.

'You've had a hard walk. Come on in, quick, and get warm. I've been expecting you.'

Though puzzled by his words – there were several other bed-and-breakfasts she could equally well have chosen – still Akiko appreciated the warmth of the hearth after the cold wind's buffeting, and she didn't let it bother her unduly.

Old man Toyokichi and Akiko were the only two guests that night. The gregarious old man showed Akiko his sketchbook and enter-tained her with anecdotes about the places he'd visited.

'I've brought a sketchbook with me too, but I don't expect I'll get anything done,' Akiko said in ingratiating tones.

'Never mind if it's not the best, go ahead and draw. That's splen-did – shall we keep each other company tomorrow?'

Toyokichi was delighted. As Akiko declined the offer in a polite murmur she took a closer look at the old man's sketchbook. Though the lines were drawn with a practised hand, the landscapes were flat; in short, he wasn't terribly good. It was, she learned, a pastime he had taken up after retirement. When she understood that the old man was just a Sunday painter, Akiko relaxed and began to comment on his sketches. Before long she even produced a snapshot of her daughter.

'I've never left her before, and I simply can't stop worrying. I wanted to get away by myself, and you'd think I'd be relieved, but no – I guess mothers are like that.' At the end of this little speech, Akiko had even heaved a convincingly lonely sigh.

Toyokichi had nodded as if much moved, and went on to talk about his grandchildren. But what had he been thinking, deep down?

After dining together they were retiring to their rooms when at the foot of the stairs old man Toyokichi silently pointed out a back room that she hadn't seen from the entrance hall. On display was an old set of Girls' Festival dolls. The emperor and empress under their dingy canopy of silk gauze struck her as a little spooky. Akiko turned back to the old man.

'They observe the festival here according to the lunar calendar. Doesn't it remind you of your daughter all over again?'

'Oh yes. If only I'd known. I should have brought her,' said Akiko, not meaning it. The old man was nodding and smiling.

The next day, embarrassed by her performance in playing up to the old man, Akiko got ready early and went downstairs hoping to miss him. There he was beside the hearth, smoking a cigarette.

And so in the end they had followed the same route all morning. They walked the mountain road, viewed a famous temple, and rode the cable car down from there. Just before they parted company the old man offered to take Akiko's photo.

'Give my regards to your daughter. You must long to be home by now – don't you wish you could fly? I envy you, having a place like that to go to.'

'Even if it's only taught me it's no fun being away from my daughter, it's been worth it.'

'I'm sure it has. Take good care of her.'

She had smilingly agreed and taken leave of the old man, who had plans to walk farther in the mountains. Akiko hadn't opened her sketchbook once. It seemed a bore to go straight back to her husband and child, yet she headed home as if to honour a promise made to the old man. She couldn't remember what reception she'd had from her daughter, nor how she herself had acted.

Some time later Toyokichi had sent her the colour photograph.

That was when she first learned his name. It had an old-fashioned ring that both she and her husband thought was quaint.

'Well, there's a nice boyfriend for you,' her husband teased, and Akiko replied, enjoying the game, 'That's right. It must be the radiant beauty of mother love that does it.'

And from then on they had exchanged New Year's greetings.

The first year she'd gone into the details of life with her daughter and even added, 'I hope we'll have an opportunity to see you.' The old man's card was much less personal.

The following year she'd energetically reported how, with her daughter started at kindergarten, she'd been able to take on a little office work.

She'd forgotten what she wrote the third year, and the fourth. Having become friendly with Kawamura at her part-time job, before she knew what had come over her she had responded to his desire, then had taken her daughter and walked in on Kawamura's home, with her husband in pursuit begging for her return; to this Kawamura replied that it hadn't been his idea and he was being imposed on himself, while Akiko looked on and cried, then faced shrieks of accusation from Kawamura's invalid wife; after a number of these scenes her daughter had gone home with her husband and they had agreed formally to a divorce. She hadn't wanted Toyokichi to receive the tiniest hint of these ugly developments. No doubt her messages had said no more than 'My daughter is growing tall. I'd like to go on another sketching trip, but it's not easy to get away.'

Her fifth card – last year's – had been briefer still, informing him only that she was well and that her name had changed. The life she was leading by then, in Kawamura's arms, was quiet in its own way, yet it appalled her to discover that she was hardened enough to make herself comfortable anywhere. Just like that nursery rhyme: 'Waking from a dream I rose, and found another dream world there.' She had a feeling that one day, like a pod bursting, her world would fly apart and her old life in the housing estate would resume.

Akiko was big with eight months' pregnancy.

And this year she hadn't sent a card. She'd even begun to think back wistfully to the woman she'd been when, six years earlier, she had affected a pious motherliness for old man Toyokichi; she was afraid of writing something that would betray the Akiko he'd met. If she could have seen him in person, she'd have liked to reveal herself wholly as she was now, smile, and say, 'This is what has become of me. It's strange, you know – the children have become very dear to me because of everything that's happened. I'm so grateful, now, that I'm a mother.' This time, Toyokichi would be truly convinced; she could see him slowly nodding.

Back in bed, Akiko went on giving the old man an account of the past six years.

In the morning she was woken by the weight of the baby. He had climbed onto her stomach and was eagerly fumbling with her pyjama top.

'You're tickling. What are you up to? If it's a feed you're after, it's all gone. Sorry.'

She picked up the baby, stripped off his wet things, and let him stay bare. She drew back the curtains, whose orange tones had grown warm, and the morning light streamed in. The sky was a dazzling solid blue.

'Ah, that feels good. Who's for sunbathing?'

Akiko slid open the glass doors. A warm earthy-smelling breeze wandered in. She opened the doors fully, inviting the wind into the room. The washing swam and the pages of the evening newspaper lifted one by one into the air. The naked baby, taking the wind against his whole body, let out a laugh.

The figure of old man Toyokichi appeared in the wind: a rucksack on his back, eyes fixed on the road, he strode away. The cedar forest on the mountain slopes creaked with each gust, and the sound echoed overhead like wild animals howling. She could make out broken tree trunks, no match for the wind's strength. One or two had fallen across the road. The gritty blasts made it impossible to keep her eyes open more than a fraction. Into this hazy field of view the figure of old man Toyokichi had sprung from behind her to vanish again before her eyes. The wind seemed to eddy after him.

Akiko held the baby's hands and stood him up.

'Wind. This thing you can't see is the wind. Now you say it: *w-i-n-d*.'

The baby opened his mouth and started to cry. She remembered that he hadn't had his morning bottle.

'Sorry, sorry! You're starving, aren't you?'

As she spoke Akiko couldn't help laughing with an irrepressible pleasure. If she were to pay Toyokichi a visit unannounced, with this baby in her arms, she'd love to see his face when he welcomed her.

In the kitchen the calendar was dancing gaily, stirred by the wind.

THE · SILENT · TRADERS

There was a cat in the wood. Not such an odd thing, really: wildcats, pumas, and lions all come from the same family and even a tabby shouldn't be out of place. But the sight was unsettling. What was the creature doing there? When I say 'wood', I'm talking about Rikugien, an Edo-period landscape garden in my neighbourhood. Perhaps 'wood' isn't quite the right word, but the old park's trees – relics of the past amid the city's modern buildings – are so overgrown that the pathways skirting its walls are dark and forbidding even by day. It does give the impression of a wood; there's no other word for it. And the cat, I should explain, didn't look wild. It was just a kitten, two or three months old, white with black patches. It didn't look at all ferocious – in fact it was a dear little thing. There was nothing to fear. And yet I was taken aback, and I tensed as the kitten bristled and glared in my direction.

The kitten was hiding in a thicket beside the pond, where my ten-year-old daughter was the first to spot it. By the time I'd made out the elusive shape and exclaimed 'Oh, you're right!' she was off calling at the top of her voice: 'There's another! And here's one over here!' My other child, a boy of five, was still hunting for the first kitten, and as his sister went on making one discovery after another he stamped his feet and wailed 'Where? Where is it?' His sister beckoned him to bend down and showed him triumphantly where to find the first cat. Several passers-by, hearing my daughter's shouts, had also been drawn into the search. There were many strollers in the park that Sunday evening. The cats were everywhere, each concealed in its own clump of bushes. Their eyes followed people's feet on the gravelled walk, and at the slightest move toward a hiding place the cat would scamper away. Looking down from an adult's height it was hard enough to detect them at all, let alone keep count, and this gave the impression of great numbers.

I could hear my younger child crying. He had disappeared while my back was turned. As I looked wildly around, my daughter pointed him out with a chuckle: 'See where he's got to!' There he was, huddled tearfully in the spot where the first kitten had been. He'd burst in eagerly, but succeeded only in driving away the kitten and trapping himself in the thicket.

'What do you think you're doing? It'll never let *you* catch it.' Squatting down, my daughter was calling through the bushes. 'Come on out, silly!'

His sister's tone of amusement was no help to the boy at all. He was terrified in his cobwebbed cage of low-hanging branches where no light penetrated.

'That's no use. You go in and fetch him out.' I gave her shoulder a push.

'He got himself in,' she grumbled, 'so why can't he get out?' All the same, she set about searching for an opening. Crouching, I watched the boy through the thick foliage and waited for her to reach him.

'How'd he ever get in there? He's really stuck,' she muttered as she circled the bushes uncertainly, but a moment later she'd broken through to him, forcing a way with both hands.

When they rejoined me, they had dead leaves and twigs snagged all over them.

After an attempt of her own to pick one up, my daughter understood that life in the park had made these tiny kittens quicker than ordinary strays and too wary to let anyone pet them. Explaining this to her brother, she looked to me for agreement. 'They were born here, weren't they? They belong here, don't they? Then I wonder if their mother's here too?'

The children scanned the surrounding trees once again.

'She may be,' I said, 'but she'd stay out of sight, wouldn't she? Only the kittens wander about in the open. Their mother's got more sense. I'll bet she's up that tree or somewhere like that where nobody

36

can get at her. She's probably watching us right now.'

I cast an eye at the treetops as I spoke – and the thought of the unseen mother cat gave me an uncomfortable feeling. Whether these were alley cats that had moved into the park or discarded pets that had survived and bred, they could go on multiplying in the wood – which at night was empty of people – and be perfectly at home.

It is exactly twenty-five years since my mother came to live near Rikugien with her three children, of which I, at ten, was the youngest. She told us the park's history, and not long after our arrival we went inside to see the garden. In spite of its being on our doorstep we quickly lost interest, however, since the grounds were surrounded by a six-foot brick wall with a single gate on the far side from our house. A Japanese garden was not much fun for children anyway, and we never went again as a family. I was reminded that we lived near a park, though, because of the many birds – the blue magpies, Eastern turtledoves, and tits – that I would see on the rooftops and in trees. And in summer I'd hear the singing of evening cicadas. To a city child like me, evening cicadas and blue magpies were a novelty.

I visited Rikugien with several classmates when we were about to leave elementary school, and someone hit on the idea of making a kind of time capsule. We'd leave it buried for ten years – or was it twenty? I've also forgotten what we wrote on the piece of paper that we stuffed into a small bottle and buried at the foot of a pine on the highest ground in the garden. I expect it's still there as I haven't heard of it since, and now whenever I'm in Rikugien I keep an eye out for the landmark, but I'm only guessing. We were confident of knowing exactly where to look in years to come, and if I can remember that so clearly it's puzzling that I can't recognize the tree. I'm not about to dig any holes to check, however – not with my own children watching. The friends who left this sentimental reminder were soon to part, bound for different schools. Since then, of course, we've ceased to think of one another, and I'm not so sure now that the bottle episode ever happened.

The following February my brother (who was close to my own age) died quite suddenly of pneumonia. Then in April my sister went to college and, not wanting to be left out, I pursued her new interests myself: I listened to jazz, went to movies, and was friendly toward college and high school students of the opposite sex. An older girl introduced me to a boy from senior high and we made up a foursome for an outing to the park – the only time I got all dressed up for Riku-gien. I was no beauty, though, nor the popular type, and while the others were having fun I stayed stiff and awkward, and was bored. I would have liked to be as genuinely impressed as they were, viewing the landscape garden for the first time, but I couldn't work up an interest after seeing the trees over the brick wall every day. By that time we'd been in the district for three years, and the name 'Rikugien' brought to mind not the tidy, sunlit lawns seen by visitors, but the dark tangles along the walls.

My desire for friends of the opposite sex was short-lived. Boys couldn't provide what I wanted, and what boys wanted had nothing to do with me.

While I was in high school, one day our ancient spitz died. The house remained without a dog for a while, until Mother was finally prompted to replace him when my sister's marriage, soon after her graduation, left just the two of us in an unprotected home. She found someone who let her have a terrier puppy. She bought a brush and comb and began rearing the pup with the best of care, explaining that it came from a clever hunting breed. As it grew, however, it failed to display the expected intelligence and still behaved like a puppy after six months; and besides, it was timid. What it did have was energy as, yapping shrilly, it frisked about the house all day long. It may have been useless but it was a funny little fellow. Its presence made all the difference to me in my intense boredom at home. After my brother's death, my mother (a widow since I was a baby) passed her days as if at a wake. We saw each other only at mealtimes, and then we seldom spoke. In high school a fondness for the movies was about the worst I could have been accused of, but Mother had no patience with such frivolity and would snap angrily at me from time to time. 'I'm leaving home as soon as I turn eighteen,' I'd retort. I meant it, too.

It was at that time that we had the very sociable dog. I suppose I'd spoiled it as a puppy, for now it was always wanting to be let in, and when I slid open the glass door it would bounce like a rubber ball right into my arms and lick my face and hands ecstatically.

38

Mother, however, was dissatisfied. She'd had enough of the barking; it got on her nerves. Then came a day when the dog went missing. I thought it must have got out of the yard. Two or three days passed and it didn't return – it hadn't the wit to find the way home once it had strayed. I wondered if I should contact the pound. Concern finally drove me to break our usual silence and ask Mother: 'About the dog . . . ' 'Oh, the dog?' she replied. 'I threw it over the wall of Rikugien the other day.'

I was shocked – I'd never heard of disposing of a dog like that. I wasn't able to protest, though. I didn't rush out to comb the park, either. She could have had it destroyed, yet instead she'd taken it to the foot of the brick wall, lifted it in her arms, and heaved it over. It wasn't large, only about a foot long, and thus not too much of a handful even for Mother.

Finding itself tossed into the wood, the dog wouldn't have crept quietly into hiding. It must have raced through the area barking furiously, only to be caught at once by the caretaker. Would the next stop be the pound? But there seemed to me just a chance that it hadn't turned out that way. I could imagine the wood by daylight, more or less: there'd be a lot of birds and insects, and little else. The pond would be inhabited by a few carp, turtles, and catfish. But what transformations took place at night? As I didn't dare stay beyond closing time to see for myself, I wondered if anyone could tell of a night spent in the park till the gates opened in the morning. There might be goings-on that by day would be unimaginable. Mightn't a dog entering that world live on, not as a tiny terrier, but as something else?

I had to be thankful that the dog's fate left that much to the imagination.

From then on I turned my back on Rikugien more firmly than ever. I was afraid of the deep wood, so out of keeping with the city: it was the domain of the dog abandoned by my mother.

In due course I left home, a little later than I'd promised. After a good many more years I moved back to Mother's neighbourhood – back to the vicinity of the park – with a little daughter and a baby. Like my own mother, I was one who couldn't give my children the experience of a father. That remained the one thing I regretted.

Living in a cramped apartment, I now appreciated the Rikugien wood for its greenery and open spaces. I began to take the children there occasionally. Several times, too, we released pet turtles or goldfish into the pond. Many nearby families who'd run out of room for aquarium creatures in their overcrowded apartments would slip them into the pond to spend the rest of their lives at liberty.

Rocks rose from the water here and there, and each was studded with turtles sunning themselves. They couldn't have bred naturally in such numbers. They must have been the tiny turtles sold at fairground stalls and pet shops, grown up without a care in the world. More of them lined the water's edge at one's feet. No doubt there were other animals on the increase – goldfish, loaches, and the like. Multi-storeyed apartment buildings were going up around the wood in quick succession, and more living things were brought down from their rooms each year. Cats were one animal I'd overlooked, though. If tossing out turtles was common practice, there was no reason why cats shouldn't be dumped here, and dogs too. No type of pet could be ruled out. But to become established in any numbers they'd have to escape the caretaker's notice and hold their own against the wood's other hardy inhabitants. Thus there'd be a limit to survivors: cats and reptiles, I'd say.

Once I knew about the cat population, I remembered the dog my mother had thrown away, and I also remembered my old fear of the wood. I couldn't help wondering how the cats got by from day to day.

Perhaps they relied on food left behind by visitors – but all of the park's litter baskets were fitted with mesh covers to keep out the crows, whose numbers were also growing. For all their nimbleness, even cats would have trouble picking out the scraps. Lizards and mice were edible enough. But on the other side of the wall lay the city and its garbage. After dark, the cats would go out foraging on the streets.

Then, too, there was the row of apartment towers along one side of the wood, facing the main road. All had balconies that overlooked the park. The climb would be quick work for a cat, and if its favourite food were left outside a door it would soon come back regularly. Something told me there must be people who put out food: there'd be elderly tenants and women living alone. Even children. Children captivated by a secret friendship with a cat.

I don't find such a relationship odd – perhaps because it occurs so often in fairy stories. But to make it worth their while the apartment children would have to receive something from the cat; otherwise they wouldn't keep it up. There are tales of mountain men and villagers who traded a year's haul of linden bark for a gallon and a half of rice in hard cakes. No villager could deal openly with the lone mountain men; so great was their fear of each other, in fact, that they avoided coming face to face. Yet when a bargain was struck, it could not have been done more skilfully. The trading was over in a flash, before either man had time to catch sight of the other or hear his voice. I think everyone wishes privately that bargains could be made like that. Though there would always be the fear of attack, or discovery by one's own side.

Supposing it were my own children: what could they be getting in return? They'd have no use for a year's stock of linden bark. Toys, then, or cakes. I'm sure they want all sorts of things, but not a means of support like linden bark. What, then? Something not readily available to them; something the cat has in abundance and to spare.

The children leave food on the balcony. And in return the cat provides them with a father. How's that for a bargain? Once a year, male cats procreate; in other words, they become fathers. They become father ad nauseam. But these fathers don't care how many children they have – they don't even notice that they are fathers. Yet the existence of offspring makes them so. Fathers who don't know their own children. Among humans, it seems there's an understanding that a man only becomes a father when he recognises the child as his own; but that's a very narrow view. Why do we allow the male to divide children arbitrarily into two kinds, recognised and unrecognised? Wouldn't it be enough for the child to choose a father when necessary from among suitable males? If the children decide that the tom that climbs up to their balcony is their father, it shouldn't cause him any inconvenience. A father looks in on two of his children from the balcony every night. The two human children faithfully leave out food to make it so. He comes late, when they are fast asleep, and they never see him or hear his cries. It's enough that they know in the morning that he's been. In their dreams, the children are hugged to their cat-father's breast.

41

We'd seen the children's human father six months earlier, and together we'd gone to a transport museum they wanted to visit. This came about only after many appeals from me. If the man who was their father was alive and well on this earth, I wanted the children to know what he looked like. To me, the man was unforgettable: I was once preoccupied with him, obsessed with the desire to be where he was; nothing had changed when I tried having a child, and I'd had the second with him cursing me. To the children, however, especially the younger one, he was a mere shadow in a photograph that never moved or spoke. As the younger child turned three, then four, I couldn't help being aware of that fact. This was the same state that I'd known myself, for my own father had died. If he had been dead it couldn't have been helped. But as long as he was alive I wanted them to have a memory of their father as a living, breathing person whose eyes moved, whose mouth moved and spoke.

On the day, he was an hour late for our appointment. The long wait in a coffee shop had made the children tired and cross, but when they saw the man a shy silence came over them. 'Thanks for coming,' I said with a smile. I couldn't think what to say next. He asked 'Where to?' and stood to leave at once. He walked alone, while the children and I looked as though it was all the same to us whether he was there or not. On the train I still hadn't come up with anything to say. The children kept their distance from the man and stared nonchalantly out of the window. We got off the train like that, and again he walked ahead.

The transport museum had an actual bullet-train carriage, steam locomotives, aeroplanes, and giant panoramic layouts. I remembered enjoying a class trip there while at school myself. My children, too, dashed excitedly around the exhibits without a moment's pause for breath. It was 'Next I want to have a go on that train', 'Now I want to work that model'. They must have had a good two hours of fun. In the meantime we lost sight of the man. Wherever he'd been, he showed up again when we'd finished our tour and arrived back at the entrance. 'What'll we do?' he asked, and I suggested giving the children a drink and sitting down somewhere. He nodded and went ahead to look for a place near the museum. The children were clinging to me as before. He entered a coffee shop that had a cake counter and I followed with them. We sat down, the three of us facing the man. Neither child showed the slightest inclination to sit beside him. They had orange drinks.

I was becoming desperate for something to say. And weren't there one or two things he'd like to ask me? Such as how the children had been lately. But to bring that up, unasked, might imply that I wanted him to watch with me as they grew. I'd only been able to ask for this meeting because I'd finally stopped feeling that way. Now it seemed we couldn't even exchange such polite remarks as 'They've grown' or 'I'm glad they're well' without arousing needless suspicions. It wasn't supposed to be like this, I thought in confusion, unable to say a word about the children. He was indeed their father, but not a father who watched over them. As far as he was concerned the only children he had were the two borne by his wife. Agreeing to see mine was simply a favour on his part, for which I could only be grateful.

If we couldn't discuss the children, there was literally nothing left to say. We didn't have the kind of memories we could reminisce over; I wished I could forget the things we'd done as if it had all been a dream, for it was the pain that we remembered. Inquiring after his family would be no better. His work seemed the safest subject, yet if I didn't want to stay in touch I had to think twice about this, too.

The man and I listened absently as the children entertained themselves.

On the way out the man bought a cake which he handed to the older child, and then he was gone. The children appeared relieved, and with the cake to look forward to they were eager to get home. Neither had held the man's hand or spoken to him. I wanted to tell them that there was still time to run after him and touch some part of his body, but of course they wouldn't have done it.

I don't know when there will be another opportunity for the children to see the man. They may never meet him again, or they may have a chance two or three years from now. I do know that the man and I will probably never be completely indifferent to each other. He's still on my mind in some obscure way. Yet there's no point in confirming this feeling in words. Silence is essential. As long as we maintain silence, and thus avoid trespassing, we leave open the possibility of resuming negotiations at any time.

43

I believe the system of bartering used by the mountain men and the villagers was called 'silent trade'. I am coming to understand that there was nothing extraordinary in striking such a silent bargain for survival. People trying to survive – myself, my mother, and my children, for example – can take some comfort in living beside a wood. We toss various things in there and tell ourselves that we haven't thrown them away, we've set them free in another world, and then we picture the unknown woodland to ourselves and shudder with fear or sigh fondly. Meanwhile the creatures multiplying there gaze stealthily at the human world outside; at least I've yet to hear of anything attacking from the wood.

Some sort of silent trade is taking place between the two sides. Perhaps my children really have begun dealings with a cat who lives in the wood.

THE · CHRYSANTHEMUM · BEETLE

Because Kazuko glanced up at the ceiling, Izumi tipped her head back and did the same. Fixed directly to the rough white surface was a white plastic case containing two fluorescent tubes. The light they provided for the large area serving as living room, dining room and kitchen was not at all dazzling even when she gazed straight at them.

'Dim in here, isn't it?' Kazuko laughed. Izumi nodded. It felt rather as if the room had suddenly darkened.

'It's a disgrace. We've been here four years and I've never once taken that cover off for a cleaning. The screens don't keep the insects out, and it beats me how they find their way into the cover, but they've gone on piling up dead, year after year. I've been meaning to get around to it all this time, and here we are, it's been four years already.'

The room overlooked a park. Although the park was on the other

* Ghost stories thrive in Japan. Before air conditioning, they were traditionally popular in summer for their chilling effect, and television variety shows still present the old favourites today. The ghost is often a wronged woman crying vengeance. In one of the most famous stories, the basis of a Kabuki play and films, the servant Okiku is put to death for breaking one of the household's treasured dishes, which her ghost can then be heard counting over and over again. There are many lesser-known versions of Okiku's story, one of which is developed here.

In the Himeji district the chrysalis of a species of butterfly is known as an *Okikumushi* (Okiku insect) from its resemblance to a female figure with arms bound behind her back; folklore has it that Okiku's spirit has taken insect form. A 1796 account from near Osaka tells of a swarm of beetles that emerged from the well in which Okiku had died one hundred years before. These insects' features are referred to in 'The Chrysanthemum Beetle.'

Judging by a recently advertised bus tour which included a visit to 'Okiku's grave', her memory has an enduring fascination. (G.H.)

45

side of the road, the cherry trees in full leaf along its fence were of a fair height and from Kazuko's third-floor apartment appeared so close that one could almost reach out and grasp the tips of their branches. The mercury-vapour lamps that lit the park must have been set back some distance, for their diffuse light blinked behind dark foliage. A busy shopping street lay on the far side, according to Kazuko, but its lights could not be seen.

'You do get a lot of insects, don't you?' Izumi remarked as she brought her gaze back from the night outside to the white fixture on the ceiling. Three narrow grooves ran the length of the cover, and on them was centred a grimy black shadow. Once she knew what it was she did get the impression that the dots furthest from the grooves were tiny insect shapes with transparent wings and spindly legs.

'Cicadas come flying smack into the screens, too.'

'Really? In the middle of Tokyo? That's amazing.'

'I'd rather have them than those hawkmoths, anyway. These may only be tiny flies, but now that I've let so many dead bodies pile up I'm scared to look. At first I simply couldn't be bothered, but for the last year or so I honestly haven't liked to open it up. I suppose I'll have to clean it out sooner or later, though.'

She finished inspecting the ceiling and topped up Izumi's beer. Kazuko's six-year-old daughter was already asleep in the next room. Izumi had timed her visit for after the little girl's bedtime, as Kazuko recommended. It was six months since they'd seen each other.

'It brings back memories, hearing about moths and cicadas and things. Hawkmoths used to stray into our house sometimes, even when I was in my teens. These days, with all these concrete buildings, there's not an ant to be seen.'

'We used to find slugs and crickets in the kitchen and hear mice scrabbling in the attic,' chuckled Kazuko, who'd been at the same high school in Tokyo twenty years ago.

'We didn't make a fuss, except about hawkmoths. For some reason it was generally dinner time when one of them flew in, and there'd be merry hell. We had to turn out the lights and fetch wet newspapers and we couldn't sit down until someone caught it.'

'They've got nasty powdery wings, haven't they? My little girl can't stand cabbage butterflies either. She bursts into tears when one

46

comes near her.'

Izumi laughed. 'Then there were always the drone beetles. Catching them was just like picking up grains of rice. I'd give their heads a good twist and flick them back outside. Though – come to think of it – I once went in for collecting the dead ones and counting them every night.' Izumi's voice brightened as the scene came to mind. 'You know how late we used to stay up in our last year at school. Well, my room was upstairs, and the desk lamp attracted swarms of flying ants. They were such a pest. I couldn't ignore them so I swatted any that sat on my hand or landed on my exercise book, till one day it occurred to me that I must have killed quite a number. And I started wondering how many. I suppose that was what started me saving up the ants I killed, all in one place. When I kept count I got a surprise, and out of a peculiar sort of curiosity I took to seeing how many I could get. Just let a winged ant come near my desk and – pow! I seem to remember a little mound of the dead ones beside my exercise books – that's how many there were. Winged ants have such dried-up bodies, I suppose it felt a bit like sweeping eraser crumbs into a pile. No, that's not quite true. I could see it was a pretty strange interest and I was doing myself no good getting in so deep. Every time my eye fell on the ants heaped at my elbow I had to stop and count them, one, two, three, and all the while I was gloating over my tally. Though it was utterly useless.' Izumi smiled at Kazuko.

Kazuko wore an expression familiar from their schooldays, her lips screwed up on the right showing her teeth in a little grimace. 'So that's the sort of thing you got up to? Oh well, it's rather typical of you, in a way.'

'Is it?' Izumi tried to recall what she'd been like at school, but couldn't pin anything down. Kazuko, who hadn't been a close friend then, had impressed her as a bold kind of girl but appeared to have nobody at school in whom she confided.

'Yes, indeed,' said Kazuko. 'Everyone used to talk about the way you got changed for swimming. While the others in the locker room were shyly shuffling out of their clothes you stripped right off first and put on your bathing suit in comfort.'

'Whatever has that got to do with winged ants?'

Izumi's laughter brought a wry smile from Kazuko. 'There does seem to be a connection,' she said.

' . . . I was shy too, you know. But I was stubborn. What are you ashamed of, I wanted to know, when we're all girls and it's so much simpler this way?'

'It's the same thing. Being stubborn, getting caught up in an emotion. Getting in too deep, in other words.'

Izumi looked at Kazuko's face. ' . . . In that case, what about yourself? . . . Wasn't that what you did?'

' . . . But I wasn't intending to have a baby from the start,' Kazuko replied, staring at the palm of her hand.

'Something made you get more and more deeply involved, didn't it? Not the baby, and not him either . . . '

Kazuko didn't answer at once.

'Well, that's one way of looking at it,' she said at length. 'Since his wife wasn't the type to lose her head, I may have wanted to know how she *would* take it. If she hadn't been so tolerant of her husband's affair, perhaps I wouldn't have had the baby . . . It's hard work making someone jealous.'

'I'd have thought it was easy.'

'As long as it's not important, yes. But when you brace yourself for a showdown, nothing happens. I longed for a scene, for his wife to burst in here on the rampage with a knife in her hand . . . I'd sigh over those stories when I saw them in the papers. When you think about it, though, she may have been longing for me to do the same. Not longing, exactly, but clinging to a hope . . . '

Izumi shifted her gaze beyond the glass doors of the balcony as she said, 'What it comes down to, in fact, is that no one wants to be killed out of jealousy. Or there'd be murders everywhere.'

Kazuko was also gazing out at the trees. ' . . . True, but there comes a time when – without knowing how you reached that point – you're convinced that's really the only thing left. Not that you want to be killed, but the time comes when you suddenly know you *have* been . . . You can't drop your guard.'

A quarter of an hour's walk from Kazuko's was the apartment where Izumi lived with her mother. Kazuko had her rent paid by the man who was her daughter's father, while Izumi and her mother owned

48

theirs, for when a developer had talked them into selling their house her mother had said forlornly that she'd rather not live on the same land and, taking her at her word, Izumi had decided on an apartment she had spotted for sale on the main road. If she couldn't leave her mother, at least she could have a change of scene. Though the new apartment was barely a stone's throw from the old place, the move did mean they shopped at a different set of stores and passed new people in the street; best of all, in Izumi's view, the main thoroughfare was brightly lit till late at night and the people going by on foot, in buses and in cars, were not all locals – all very different from the quiet residential area they had left. Her mother soon regretted the move as the traffic noise disturbed her, but Izumi would gladly take the traffic noise rather than let age creep up on her while she listened to the neighbours' laughter and ringing phones, doors opening and shutting, and the whirr of washing machines.

The house where Kazuko's parents lived was not far either. From the station, which was on the Yamanote Line, Kazuko's parents' house lay to the north; to the south, the first road on the right led to where Izumi had formerly lived, while the left turn at the same crossroads followed the railway line down a sunless slope; halfway along the slope there was a flight of stone steps, from the top of which it was a short walk to Kazuko's. Izumi's new apartment was due south of the station, just to the left of the large intersection. She occasionally saw Kazuko or her parents at the station. In any case there was nothing unusual in coming across faces familiar since childhood. They wouldn't stop and talk, of course, but the sight of these people was enough to give her a sinking feeling: why on earth couldn't they launch out and live somewhere else?

A number of other tenants in the building where Izumi and her mother had settled turned out to be people born and bred in the district, though none of their faces was actually familiar. After the promise of a move to a brand-new building, to Izumi's disappointment she often found herself sharing the elevator with elderly people. They had come back from wherever they'd lived in their prime to end their days in the place where they were born. If that was why they'd come, said Izumi's mother, she supposed they were happy to be here, noise or no noise. Having ample opportunity to talk to the other old

49

people, she passed on to Izumi what she'd learned, scornful and envious by turns.

The job of caretaker had fallen to the wife of the real estate agent on the first floor. When told the business had been in the family for two generations, Izumi did vaguely recall the sombre wooden house that had stood on the site. There had been an apartment upstairs, so the family must have lived in the gloomy rooms behind the office. When the old father had died the eldest son had succeeded him and turned his knowledge of the trade to account by promptly putting up a tall, narrow apartment building. He established the second of eight floors as his family's home, and rented out space for a small shop at street level alongside their own office premises. The eldest son was close to forty, and his wife, who was small, thin, and plainly dressed, would have been about Izumi's age. They had two children, girls who took after their father, both at elementary school. At first the tenants were told an outside firm would supply a janitor, but when no suitable applicant could be found the agent's wife had ended up doing the job herself. At work among the garbage cans in the lobby, she certainly didn't look too happy about it. She appeared to be grumbling that she hadn't the strength as she organised the stacks of newspapers left out by tenants or washed plastic rubbish pails big enough to contain her.

A man showed up each day in the agent's office. At times he was seen taking the woman's place – hauling the full pails out to the street or mopping the lobby floor. He kept his face lowered and pretended not to notice any of the tenants who passed through. Glimpsed from the side, his features wore the sulky look of a child forced to do as he's told, helping his parents with hated chores. He was another who couldn't escape the old central city district of his birth. His name was Takashi. He was the agent's younger brother, who had left home for a time to live on the outskirts of Tokyo but returned when the apartment block was built. As Izumi learned a year or so after she moved in, he rented cheap rooms nearby and lived alone.

Early in their acquaintance, Izumi had asked: 'You have dinner at your brother's, don't you? Does his wife cook? Or does your mother?'

She'd caught sight of his mother from time to time, shopping in the neighbourhood, and she regularly came across the daughter-in-law at the butcher's or the fish shop. At the thought of him being fed by his

50

mother or sister-in-law, whichever it might be, she couldn't help drawing a comparison with herself eating meals cooked by her mother at much the same age as Takashi, and she wanted to make quite sure he knew that she didn't owe her job, at least, to any such arrangement.

Perhaps Takashi caught the hint of sarcasm in her inquiry, for he answered with a rancour that startled her. 'I don't go to their goddamn place. Why the hell should I?'

'I just thought you must get on well since you help your brother in his work. Anyone would think so, wouldn't they? It's better than people thinking you're on bad terms,' said Izumi, unabashed. They were in a bar near the station.

'I could be a complete stranger for all anybody knows.'

' . . . But your brother's family don't think so, and that's what counts. It must save them a lot of trouble having a brother in the business, and I'm sure the fact that you were born here must have encouraged you to come back?'

'I simply thought I could use them. That's all they're good for, the lot of them,' Takashi muttered, this time without expression.

'Huh. I've no way of knowing if that's true. But if you're out to use them, you should use them for everything you can get. If it's only talk, it makes you look pretty silly.'

Izumi shrank momentarily from Takashi's glance, then forced a smile. She couldn't be sure whether Takashi was an easy man to handle or a difficult one, and not knowing was so unsettling that she just couldn't keep quiet. Only when some remark of hers had succeeded in needling Takashi could she begin to relax at last. A nagging older sister might feel as she did – suddenly tempted to laugh when her brother rewarded her with a glare, a pout and a protest.

She had run into Takashi in the street one night. Recognising him from her building, she had smiled and nodded a greeting. At this, Takashi had stopped and asked, 'Do you have to go straight home?' smiling vaguely at her. Izumi was on her way home from an office party, and it was after ten. Takashi, in sandals, was heading towards the station. Not immediately seeing the point of the question, Izumi had answered 'No' with equal friendliness. 'In that case,' said Takashi with the same vague expression, 'how about joining me for a drink somewhere nearby?' Izumi had nodded without hesitation: 'All right, then, but not for long.'

Over their drinks, Takashi had said, 'I'm on my own, but you live with your mother, don't you?'

'That's right. How did you know?' said Izumi in surprise. There was nothing strange in his knowing the tenants' affairs, as he worked beside the building's owner and helped the caretaker. Yet it had given her a moment's discomfort when a stranger drew attention point-blank to the fact that she lived with her mother.

Izumi began to explain how she'd come to live in the building.

'Really? You had a place over there?' Takashi said as if struck by a common interest. 'I know it well. A nice quiet area. I used to play there often when I was a kid. We must have gone to the same school, then?'

'No, our house was just over the school district boundary. I went to a different junior high as well. But I went to the senior high right down the street.' Izumi, too, had perked up at the mention of a subject unexpectedly close to home.

'You went there? You must be bright.'

'Not a bit. It was just the nearest.'

'I didn't go to the local high school. I took the Yamanote Line to school.'

'Then you must be smart yourself. Going out of district.'

'That was how I explained it to my parents – said I wanted to go to a more academic school so that I could study. Since my marks weren't bad for some reason, they were tickled pink. I wonder what they expected of me.'

When Izumi had asked, on this first occasion, 'Where do you live now? Still in the same place?' Takashi had chuckled at a private joke.

'What's so funny?'

Watching her perplexed expression, Takashi had spoken as if posing a riddle: 'The old house has gone, like yours. It gave way to an apartment building, which went up a year ago.'

Izumi still hadn't caught on. He kept her guessing till, losing interest, he revealed the answer: that the owner of the real estate was his brother.

Takashi had left home when he entered a university in an outlying

52

town. He'd spun out his time there to six years, then found a job with a printing company in the same prefecture. After several years there, when told his father was dying, he had come home. His father died, the apartments were built. As he'd been wanting a change, he agreed to team up with his brother, and he moved in nearby. This, as far as Izumi could draw it out of him, seemed to be the sequence of events up to their meeting.

She drank freely as Takashi offered round after round of cold saké, and she described the job she'd been doing as a buyer of imported sheet music since leaving college ten years earlier. Though not without complaints, she added that it was too late to think of doing anything else. Since Takashi didn't ask, she didn't tell him that her father – long separated from her mother – had become ill and died the year she started university, nor that she had been on the point of leaving home and abandoning her mother two or three times. Since these had never amounted to more than two or three nights away from home, they hardly qualified for a special mention.

The conversation reverted to the part of town where they lived, and they tried to outdo each other listing old classmates who lived on the same block.

When they got up to go, it was already after twelve. Outside, Takashi unhesitatingly put his arm around Izumi's shoulders and said, 'You're okay for time, aren't you?' At the nearness of Takashi's body, for the first time Izumi couldn't breathe normally, but she nodded at once in reply.

Climbing a slope, crossing a railway bridge, and turning down a narrow street, they came to a very recently built hotel with Grecian columns spaced along its facade. They were on the point of passing by as if they hadn't noticed, when Izumi peered into the discreetly scaled-down entrance and said in a teasing fashion, 'They say people come here from miles away. Someone at work told me. It's even been on one of those shows on TV. Did you know?'

'Never heard of it,' said Takashi, gazing up at the colonnaded wall.

'You know . . . ' Izumi ventured appealingly, 'I've been thinking I'd like to see inside. Why don't we go in?'

She trembled, but because she'd made the move herself before Takashi could come out with some well-worn phrase, she had managed to keep her voice steady.

'Okay. Sure you don't mind a place like this?' Takashi's reaction came easily and comfortably. He showed so little surprise at a woman's speaking first that he quite took the wind out of Izumi's sails.

In the room Takashi undressed just as comfortably, and just as easily enjoyed Izumi's body, so that later that night, back in her apartment, she decided to consider what had happened as a special time she'd enjoyed while it lasted. She too had had a good time, and that was enough.

She didn't spot Takashi the next day, although she watched out for him. Nor the next day. She remembered that she used to see him once a week, if that, as she left for work early in the morning and generally wasn't home before seven, by which time the office downstairs was closed. Unless Takashi were to pick the right moment to hang about in the lobby or near the station, it would be almost impossible to run into him on a weekday. Since she had Saturdays off and the real estate agency stayed open, she could have gotten a look at him on the job through the front windows, but she had no business that would take her past the office. Not that she wanted to meet him. If she'd felt that way she had only to call him directly, since he had given her both his work and his home phone numbers.

When several days went by with no sign of Takashi, Izumi began to have certain misgivings. How had it been possible for Takashi to invite her for a drink so simply when their paths had crossed near the station? There might have been a natural curiosity on his part, knowing as he did that Izumi was single and living with her mother. The invitation might have been a whim, a way of filling time, but even so Izumi wasn't vain enough to imagine it was her looks that had caught his passing fancy. She hadn't meant to make something of it, but a doubt was growing in her mind: what had brought her and Takashi together like that? Until then they'd never had occasion to speak, barely knew each other by sight. Izumi recalled the pleasant smile she'd given Takashi in the street. And then had to admit she hadn't been entirely disinterested herself. Without particularly intending it, she'd been watching the man who had to share the chores because the agent was too cheap to pay a janitor. A thin man, he had a pale and dry complexion, and it was hard to tell his age: his manner seemed to place him in his twenties, but his face could have been taken for forty. He seldom smiled. Once, though, she'd noticed him outside the office with a middle-aged woman – a customer, she supposed – shouting with laughter at something that must have been very funny. What had been in Izumi's eyes as she watched Takashi laughing? For he'd been aware of her gaze. And that wouldn't have been the only time; he'd been aware all along. Aware of Izumi's eyes slipping furtively away and yet always pursuing, never letting him escape her attention, watching avidly for her chance. Had he muttered, smiling tightly to himself, 'Oh, her'? The idea made Izumi stiffen with shame. At the same time she felt the man had shown himself in a sinister light. How *could* he have noticed a woman's covert gaze? Or had her eyes begun to pursue him so openly?

After two weeks, Izumi received a phone call toward midnight from Takashi. Feeling her heart beat through her whole body, she raced out. By the time she found Takashi standing at the nearest corner she was smiling palely.

They met two or three times more over the course of a month before Takashi first took Izumi to his own place. It wasn't what she'd expected when he spoke of a cheap apartment. It was in a concrete building, a small three-storeyed block, and to reach it from Izumi's they crossed the main road and walked for ten minutes through residential streets where there were still old houses, till they came to an area so secluded it struck her as gloomy. Takashi's place was on the third floor. The surrounding trees were thickly branched, suggesting the building's age. The stairs and corridor gave no hint of other people's presence. At first the rooms in the apartment impressed Izumi as spacious. To her surprise there was a permanent bed – she'd expected futons, just as she'd expected the building to be wooden. As Takashi had started taking off his clothes in the dark, Izumi also undressed. He certainly wasn't bad as a partner for obtaining physical pleasure. Thinking herself lucky in that, at least, Izumi put her arms around Takashi's clean-smelling body. Takashi always performed sex quietly, like a ceremony, never requiring of her more excitement than necessary. Izumi couldn't be content without making her own wants known, little by little, deepening her sensations.

Getting up, Takashi brought Izumi a glass of water. As she drank she had a good look around. The room was of moderate size, six tatami mats in area, but divided from the adjoining six-mat room by a curtain which was left open, giving the impression of space. The kitchen seemed bleak without a dining table in the area meant for it, although there were a large refrigerator and china cabinet.

'You must be rich to have all this to yourself.'

Takashi switched on the fluorescent lamp by the bed.

'Did you think I was poor? Not having a proper job at my age? I bet you thought I'd made a mess of things and come back here with nothing but debts. Sorry to disappoint you, but you're entirely wrong. Isn't a rich man to your liking?'

'So this is what you call rich? If I was on my own, I'd live so well you wouldn't dare come near me. I earn a good salary.'

'So do I.' Takashi laughed at his own words. 'Don't worry, I admit you've worked a lot harder than me.'

'That doesn't especially thrill me. Work, work, work – I haven't been living only for my work, you know. There was someone I was in love with, too.'

'Well, that figures. You've been out of college for ten years – plenty happens in ten years.'

'You know what? For someone who lives alone, you've got a lot of dishes. Are you fussy about housework? Look, you've even got a vacuum cleaner.'

Its hose was poking out from a corner of the kitchen. Izumi glanced at the sink. A striped cloth was spread out to dry over the long tap. A squat, pale pink thermos jug sat on the bench. She studied the china cabinet. He had just about everything. Soup bowls, meat dishes, fish plates, bread-and-butter plates, saucers. Even glass salad bowls. Teacups and lacquered soup bowls were there – two of each. She saw that the shelves in the next room also held coffee cups and glasses. The glasses were an assortment, but the coffee cups were of two kinds, paired. Besides, now that she thought about it, when she'd slipped between the sheets Takashi's bed hadn't felt as foreign as a bed should if it was being slept in every night by a lone man.

' . . . This apartment looks like someone's wife walked out on him. Were you ever married?' Izumi asked, smiling. Then, feeling a need

56

to convey that she didn't care one way or the other, she let out a yawn and began putting on her underwear.

'As a wealthy bachelor I get more offers than I can handle.' Takashi made a feeble joke and stared, smiling, at Izumi's body.

'How nice for you. Then I'm surprised I don't hear colourful gossip about you from the leisurely ladies in our building.'

'That's because over there I'm devoted to my work.'

Izumi burst out laughing. It was a relief not to have heard something more disturbing.

If in fact Izumi had noticed Takashi first, wondering what kind of man he was, and if he'd responded because she couldn't take her eyes off him, how much confidence would these developments have given him? The thought made her body tense. It also caused her to probe her own feelings: why had the sight of Takashi begun to attract her attention? Because as a resident of the building she couldn't seem to fit him into place. Because from the first she'd been off guard with him, a man on her own territory, who helped out with the chores in the building. Yet she hadn't wanted to get closer to him in a personal way. Or at least she'd never considered it. Maybe Takashi hadn't noticed anything, maybe that night he'd simply caught sight of her and thought of inviting her for a drink. Because for some time he'd secretly been aware of Izumi living alone with her mother.

She was old enough to know that the puzzle wouldn't be solved by asking Takashi himself. He would laugh the question off with some remark like 'Oh, you were so beautiful' or 'You're my type'. Izumi could even picture her own blush as she replied, 'Really?' She'd had an affair with a boy at university that had started unexpectedly, but then she'd been able, without hesitation, to pride herself on how much he must have felt for her. She'd condescended to become involved, and when she'd learned afterwards that from his point of view it had been a kind of accident due to sexual desire, she'd suffered in equal measure for her conceit. She felt a fondness for the Izumi of those days. And here she was ten years later, and her mother was unmistakably ten years further into old age. In another ten years she'd remember herself as she was now and sigh over how young she'd still been.

57

She didn't want to believe that what had prompted Takashi toward a sexual relationship was his seeing the hunger deep down in her body and, moreover, recognising her limitation: that at this late stage she wasn't going to be able to leave her mother's side.

Six months had gone by since they'd taken to having sex in Takashi's room. Then it had been the end of summer; now it was the dead of winter. Her second winter in the new apartment. It was cosier than their drafty old house, needing only a small electric heater and a foot warmer for complete comfort, but because she then forgot the wintry temperatures outdoors she'd caught cold both years. Her lingering cold may have been partly to blame for her increasing irritation with Takashi.

Over the months they had ceased to make arrangements by phone. Instead, on a particular day of the week Izumi would slip out at the agreed time, after checking that her mother was asleep, and run to Takashi's apartment. From time to time Takashi might suggest seeing a movie on the weekend and then Izumi would stay the night, and on Sunday, at her suggestion, they'd spend all afternoon at a department store gallery where Egyptian antiquities were on display, or at a weaving exhibition in which a friend had some work, or at a concert held regularly in a café. When the autumn colours were out they had strolled in Hibiya Park, near the band shell. That was the one time that Izumi had been in unconditionally high spirits, scampering after the pigeons or bursting operatically into song among the trees. As if this too were playfulness she clung to Takashi's arm and said sweetly, 'I'd love some popcorn,' and Takashi, who seemed not to mind as long as Izumi was having fun, bought her some with a wry smile. As she took handfuls from the bag, she added the final touch by resting her head archly against his shoulder and saying in a confiding whisper:

'We could be on a real date like this, couldn't we? I've always wanted to try a typical date.'

Takashi laughed and played along by stroking her head till, self-consciousness returning, he quickly shoved Izumi away.

'Behave yourself! What's "a typical date" supposed to mean?'

'Walking like lovers in the movies.' Izumi laughed uproariously.

Whenever she went to Takashi's room she was made to feel the presence of another woman, but she reprimanded herself – just because she was sexually involved, did she have to instantly turn on the silly suspicions? – and decided to take no notice. She hadn't sounded out Takashi, of course. Yet no matter how sternly she warned herself, her eyes went about their work as acutely as before. After a number of visits she could tell it wasn't her imagination. There was a women's magazine which Takashi couldn't possibly want to read on top of the stack of old newspapers in the kitchen. Two or three long hairs lay on the bathroom floor. They weren't Takashi's and Izumi's own hair was short. A bag of raisin biscuits had been stuffed into the china cabinet.

She had considered ringing or dropping in on a day when Takashi wouldn't otherwise be expecting her. But she hadn't yet even brought herself to tell Takashi that she wanted to see him on more days of the week. She was never the one who phoned, either. She'd remained on guard, knowing she'd end up at a disadvantage if she ever let herself become too attached to Takashi. That initial niggling doubt would not go away.

Izumi reminded herself that she couldn't call Takashi to account, whatever he might be doing or thinking when she wasn't there, because her own eyes were roving restlessly over Takashi's head in hopes of a man who would come if she asked him to her mother's apartment, or, failing that, at least let her complain in peace about her mother – but the next thing that those eyes fell on was two coffee mugs left upside down in the dish rack in Takashi's kitchen. Though not identical, they were of matching design, pottery with a dark blue pattern.

It was then that Izumi was first struck by something different, something she couldn't accept. In front of Takashi she kept her displeasure well hidden, but after returning home she choked and began to tremble. What was he up to? Those mugs were an exceedingly theatrical prop, no matter how she looked at it. Being Takashi, he was hardly likely to have checked carefully around his rooms in case there was anything Izumi shouldn't see. And yet he did have a fastidious streak: his sharp eyes noticed things dropped in the street, right down to ten yen coins and rubber bands. He must have been aware of those mugs whether he liked it or not. And the mugs weren't all: even if he hadn't been consciously checking, shouldn't his eyes have taken in the women's magazine, the bag of biscuits, the hairs on the bathroom tiles? She could see Takashi glance at the bathroom floor, notice the hairs, and stare at them for several seconds before laughing grimly and leaving. But that might not be the worst of it: she could also see Takashi inspect the bathroom floor, take a closer look in the waste-paper basket and under the mat where hairs tended to catch, pick out two or three which by their length were clearly a woman's and, with a grin, carefully position them in the middle of the floor. On the point of throwing out the woman's forgotten magazine with a bunch of old newspapers, he might have remembered that it was the day Izumi came and put the pile back in the kitchen, leaving the magazine on top where she couldn't miss it. What if he hadn't actually been using the mugs with the woman, either, but had deliberately taken them from the shelf and placed them in the draining rack, then gone over to the bed and surveyed the kitchen, smiling faintly? 'Yes,' he'd say, 'that'll do nicely for today.'

Nonsense, he wouldn't go that far. Izumi would have liked to dismiss her suspicions. For one thing, what was there to link either the magazine or the mugs directly with a woman? Takashi was not entirely without friends. His brother's family might be in and out, his friends might drop by freely. Perhaps, since he'd mentioned a shop owner and a teacher at a homework coaching school, one of them might even have borrowed the apartment while Takashi was out and have spent the day there with a woman.

Izumi tried to calm herself, to laugh at letting a thing like that disturb her. Because he was to be found on the first floor of her building every day, she seemed to have forgotten how to maintain a distance. He was too close at hand, and she wasn't able to draw the line in her mind any more.

But that night Izumi took a long time to go to sleep, trembling all the while.

She went on dismissing her fears as nonsense. While she was with him Takashi didn't make any comments offensive to her ears, and he showed attachment to her body. He continued holding her even after sex was over. He listened with apparent enjoyment to what she said and, for his part, talked about the old classmates who lived nearby, what they'd been like as kids and what they were doing now, or abused the teachers they'd had and chatted about those he'd liked, or told her about customers at the office, his brother, and his brother's family. As the time they spent together grew more intimate, she couldn't help wishing she could spend every weekend at Takashi's. Takashi said nothing when she closed her eyes and whispered, 'I'm so sleepy. If I go to sleep now, I wonder if I can wake up before morning?' He said neither 'Get some rest', nor 'Don't you dare'. Only when she'd reluctantly climbed out of bed and begun dressing would Takashi say with an air of relief, 'Look at the time. We'll be half asleep tomorrow,' as he also got up. Takashi had never said out loud, 'Don't come any closer.' Izumi had never said in so many words, 'I want to come a little closer.' She was convinced that they'd been able to preserve the sense of intimacy they'd had till now because she'd drawn her own line and made sure to back away when she reached it. Though she didn't draw the line gladly.

Apart from this feeling of Izumi's, however, there were definitely odd things happening in Takashi's room. After the mugs, the next was a gold chain left on the TV. Takashi would not have been caught dead wearing any sort of jewellery. While suffering the little jabs of light from the gleaming chain, Izumi pretended as usual to have noticed nothing. Next it was a stocking. The moment she caught sight of it she opened her mouth and almost uttered a sound, for there was now no denying her suspicion that he was up to something. She just managed to stop herself in time, but her agitation had not been lost on Takashi.

'What's wrong?' Takashi's voice was leisurely as he continued playing with Izumi's breasts. Izumi looked at his face. He wore a flushed, contented, childish smile.

' . . . Nothing,' she murmured, turning her face away.

'You sure? You jumped just now.' His tone was natural.

' . . . You tickled me.'

She wanted to brush his fingers from her breast and burst out – in tears perhaps – 'What is that doing there! What are you doing, you sneak! What are you thinking of!'

The stocking was rolled up, flower-shaped, in a corner of the room.

By the following week they were into March. Fine snow fell and vanished at once. Izumi felt some hesitation, but she thought better of it and went to Takashi's room, running along dark streets chilled by melted snow. There was no change in Takashi's face. She fussed about being frozen as she went inside and crouched before the kerosene heater, rubbing her hands together, making a point of how cold she was. She didn't want her gaze to travel. As soon as she was warm she wanted to get swiftly into bed. Then she would only have to see Takashi's face.

Takashi made her a cup of coffee. As she was sipping it there in front of the stove, he embarrassedly thrust out a flat paper bag.

'What's this?' Izumi asked in astonishment. She had never received anything from Takashi, not even for safekeeping. She couldn't help being wary: was this another of his weird tricks?

'Open it and see. I think you'll like it.' Takashi pressed the bag against her chest. There was enthusiasm in his voice.

Gingerly opening the paper bag, she glimpsed black woollen material with brown stripes. She pulled out a muffler which could have been a man's or a woman's.

'Hm. It's very nice. But what's it for?'

'It's a present.' Takashi nodded in satisfaction. 'Yes, it'll look good on you.'

'A present? Well, I'm delighted, but what's it *for*? This is so sudden I don't know what to make of it.' Izumi was looking first at the front, then at the back of the scarf as she spoke. She sensed danger in her impulse to unrestrained joy.

'No harm in it once in a while, is there? Isn't your birthday coming up? So it's a birthday present. To tell the truth, I had to send something to a business contact, and while I was in the department ·store I came across a bargain sale, and I found this. I don't wear scarves myself but I thought, you know, this might appeal to Izumi.'

'Whatever came over you? It's *too* kind, somehow – it scares me. But can I really have it?'

'Of course. I bought it for you.' Takashi was laughing, red-faced. The corners of his eyes were creasing into laugh lines.

'I'll try it on, then . . . ' Izumi wound the muffler around her neck. 'It's very nice. Must be good quality. It's lovely and warm.'

Izumi too was flushed. Grinning away foolishly, not knowing how else to give vent to her delight, she put her hands on Takashi's cheeks, pulled him roughly toward her, and pressed her lips to his.

They went over to the bed, their bodies tangled, and in time Izumi moved in different ways until she had the sensation that her body flew into shining transparent pieces as Takashi ejaculated, and for some time afterwards, with her hands against Takashi's chest as he too struggled for breath, she was unable to open her eyes or move.

Eventually Takashi got up and invited her into the shower. She joined him there face to face, exclaiming happily at how unsteady she was. Takashi was in a good mood, too, giving her nipples a special soaping and suddenly prodding her backside. When they'd dried off they dived back into bed and tried the muffler on each other, till Izumi was reminded of an old game and fetched her gloves to make a puppet in the way she'd done as a child, then Takashi's gloves to make another, and they played at inventing voices.

While they were occupied like this, the hour arrived for Izumi to leave. If she asked him today, she thought, mightn't he let her stay with no fuss? She wasn't keen, in fact, to go out into the cold street and run home as usual. And her mother had some inkling of the change in Izumi, so she wouldn't be seriously worried by her staying out overnight. Nevertheless, Izumi staunchly got out of bed and began putting on her underwear. She wasn't going to stay unless Takashi asked her.

Takashi said nothing as he watched Izumi dress. He had his pyjamas on by the time she was ready. The finishing touch was the scarf he'd given her. Relieved that today, anyway, she'd escaped seeing any of those suggestive feminine items, she smiled at him and said, 'Thanks for this. I was thrilled. There's another three weeks to my birthday, but I won't be polite and wait. I'll wear it right now before it gets too warm.'

'No use being polite. It's just a bargain I picked up at a sale. I'll buy you plenty more if that one makes you so happy.'

With these generous words Takashi saw Izumi to the door. He switched on the light for her in the darkened entrance as she stooped to put on her boots. Something odd caught her attention. She stared again to one side. A paper bag was propped up in the shadow of the shoe rack. It was of the same size and design as the bag that had held the muffler, and it had a similar bulge. All the blood in her body drained away, then swirled back in a violent rush. A last restraint, the one she had struggled to hold firm, gave way like a latch breaking and before she knew what she was doing she had pounced on the bag with a jarring cry, almost a scream, and torn it apart with all her might. A scarf the same as the one she had on fell softly to the floor. Izumi sank down with it, and for a moment or two writhed there emitting a strange sound.

It occurred to her to wonder what Takashi was doing, and only then did she regain her speech. She yanked the scarf from her neck, flung it on the floor, got up, and with her right fist punched him in the midriff putting all the strength in her body behind the blow. She seemed to have connected as he doubled up painfully and pulled a face.

'I've known for ages there was something fishy going on. I've kept quiet because I thought I'd be a bigger fool if I took you up on it. But you must be out of your mind to go this far. You're crazy. What would make you do such a thing? Just to get at me – it's horrible. I won't take it any more, do you hear? I was so thrilled, and all along you were laughing up your sleeve as if you'd given me poison.'

Takashi answered, looking serious and a little pale as he regarded Izumi's face streaming with tears: 'I'm no murderer.'

'What? That's not what I'm saying and you know it. I'm asking why you deliberately put this thing where I could see it. I'm not having any more to do with you so you might as well tell me whatever you want. Go on, tell me!'

Her nose was also streaming, and as the snivel ran into her mouth Izumi hurriedly wiped her face with her fingers, then slumped down on the spot. Takashi promptly sat cross-legged beside her. The two scarves were underneath him. Noticing, he drew one out and made as if to hand it to her.

' . . . But I bought it especially. So take it with you!'

'You've got to be kidding.' This time she chucked the scarf into the kitchen.

'But you were so pleased before.'

'I hadn't caught on to your nasty scheme then, as you know very well. I don't understand you. Does it make you happy to see a woman hurt?'

Izumi was shaking visibly. Though not frightened for her life, she was alarmed by Takashi's manner, which was almost unchanged in the face of her own hysteria. Did this mean that the man had really been making deliberate use of women's things all this time in order to test Izumi's reaction? Fear was churning her insides.

'Hurt? Why are you hurt? I bought it for you, Izumi. That's all there is to it, surely?'

' . . . But that – ' Keeping down the nausea, Izumi jerked her jaw a little to indicate the other scarf still under Takashi's buttocks.

'Oh, this? . . . This isn't for you, I'm afraid.'

'I know that! That's why I'm asking what made you purposely leave it here. If you mean to tell me you've got another woman, *tell* me! Properly!' Something had gone very wrong with Izumi's voice. Tears and snivel began to flow again.

'If I told you . . . you'd have simply shrugged it off.'

' . . . So you did do it on purpose, to hurt me . . . '

Takashi sighed and smiled thinly, as if hoping somehow to comfort her. 'Now why do you say that? You're talking as if you were jealous.'

'And what's wrong with that? Of course I am!' Izumi shouted, then bent her head.

'Have you ever said you loved me, or anything like it? . . . I see. How long ago did you notice?'

' . . . The magazine. That magazine.'

'Oh, that . . . It bothered you?'

Izumi nodded.

' . . . Funny, isn't it? You may think it's jealousy, but I wouldn't be so sure . . . You can meet the other woman any time you like. She seems to be worrying about you, too. Though she's taken it in a slightly different way . . . But to tell you the truth I'm relieved. You always acted so reasonable.'

' . . . You mean you wanted me to be jealous?'

'No, that's not what I mean. I don't like that word, jealous. It sounds phoney. I thought perhaps you didn't like it either. It was a worry, though, not knowing what you were really thinking . . . Well, shall I give you her phone number? I'll write it down.'

Izumi leaped up in alarm. 'No, it's all right. Don't talk like that. Stop it, will you?'

She wiped her face again with both hands before pulling on her boots. Takashi sat on the floor, silent and unmoving.

A woman – a mere girl in Izumi's eyes – stood up and bowed her head. Izumi returned the greeting and sat down at the café table.

It was exactly twenty days since she had last been to Takashi's. The following day was Izumi's birthday. Wondering if Takashi had remembered it brought back that day's terror. She was trying to mark out a breathing space for herself: she wouldn't do anything until after her birthday, anyway. The season was changing, spring was near, and that room was gradually receding. Once she'd run into Takashi by the emergency stairway in her building. He had given her a dazzled sort of smile and dipped his head. Though she hadn't managed to smile, she was able to bow her head casually. There had been no phone calls from Takashi since she stopped going to his apartment. Nor letters, of course. For that, at least, she was thankful.

The previous evening, Izumi had received a phone call from the woman. When she gave a dubious answer to the unfamiliar voice, the woman mentioned Takashi's name. 'I asked him for your telephone number,' she said politely, 'as I'd very much like to meet you.'

'But I'm no longer – ' Izumi said.

'Whatever you're going to do, I would still like to meet you, because I don't think I'll be able to give him up.'

Izumi had the feeling she'd like to meet this woman, whose name was Nobuko. They agreed to meet at seven in a coffee shop near Izumi's office. Nobuko was waiting as arranged, wearing a red sweater and holding a wristwatch in her hand. She had a square face, but engaging features – she certainly wasn't bad-looking. Young as she was, she wore her fine, straight hair in a short cut that made her seem even younger. Feeling ashamed of her own looks – which were not at all remarkable, and matched her years – Izumi couldn't help first asking Nobuko her age.

'I'm twenty-eight. But everyone sees me as awfully childish,' Nobuko answered promptly in a clear voice. She seemed to be a

66

precise person, for she began at once to talk about herself with an energy that suggested there wasn't a moment to waste.

Nobuko had met Takashi when she was twenty-two. She'd gone to junior college in a neighbouring prefecture, then worked in an office where, after four years, she'd gotten to know Takashi. He was twenty-seven. He was unpopular, the subject of much gossip where women were concerned, and a slacker on the job. Even so Nobuko couldn't take a dislike to him, couldn't bring herself to rebuff him. Takashi began to come to her lodgings.

' . . . I grew up in the country, you see, so I've been away from home since I left school,' Nobuko added apologetically.

It may not have meant as much to Takashi, but Nobuko felt a deep joy at their special relationship. Perhaps, too, like the young girl she was, she'd been reaching for too much; she'd thought Takashi far more adult and far less impulsive than he actually was. She very much wanted them to live together, but it would take three years to accomplish this. In spite of a fright he gave her when he struck up a friendship with another woman, she couldn't see Takashi as someone with strong desires, or at least she couldn't believe he had a particular fondness for the female sex in general. Unable to give up her hopes entirely, Nobuko had continued to see him. During this time a change in her circumstances, not connected with Takashi, had meant that she needed to find a new job. Her troubles continued, reducing her to such a state that she didn't often feel up to seeing Takashi. What he'd made of this she couldn't say, but one day he'd proposed they rent a place together, a little bigger than either one of them had at the time. Of course Nobuko wasn't going to refuse. When Takashi chose an apartment, she moved in before him.

Nobuko's story would clearly take time. At Izumi's suggestion, they left the coffee shop for an Italian restaurant down the street. A row of rather weary potted primroses stood along its counter. The early magnolias should be in full bloom by now, Izumi realised. Near where she used to live there was a house with a large magnolia tree, and she'd gone back this time last year especially to see it, but this year she'd forgotten all about magnolias and the like. They took a table by the window and decided what to order. Despite the impression that her face created, Nobuko was fleshy in build and

67

perhaps inclined to perspire, for tiny beads of sweat stood out in the dip beneath her nose. Remembering how little Takashi used to sweat, Izumi felt her breath catch.

'. . . But we had only a year living together. Or not quite a year, in fact,' Nobuko began again.

There were few customers, and the restaurant was quiet. Between lunchtime and evening the place was always crowded with workers from the surrounding offices, but apparently there wasn't enough business to keep it open at night, and it was showing signs of closing at an early hour. If Nobuko didn't finish here, they'd have to find somewhere else. As she listened to her, Izumi was wishing she'd chosen the restaurant with a little more care.

'He took to staying out, and when he did come home he wasn't always alone . . . After a while he left for Tokyo, because his father had died, I believe . . . But I never know when enough is enough. I found out where he was living, and persisted in writing, and even coming to Tokyo on Sundays. He never showed the slightest resentment – he was always happy to spend time with me. I felt a bit more secure after that, and decided to give it time and see what happened.

'Once a month I came and stayed Saturday night. A good many of his things were left behind in my apartment, so I brought them by degrees, and as I didn't like having the bed and the china cabinet to myself I moved them to his place. He doesn't mind that kind of thing. One way or another, after all the quarrels we'd had, I'd learned to guess what was on his mind and what worried him . . .

'But what's happened has been hard for me, too. Even though I thought I understood, I hated it. I cried and raged. Many times I yelled "Stop, why do you have to be like this?" I thought seriously of getting out. Though I'm glad now that I didn't . . . I've gotten side-tracked. Anyway, one day he said to me, "Do you suppose we could live together again?" That made me feel so smug. Looking back, though, I realise it was about the time he must have met you, Izumi.'

Nobuko broke off and studied Izumi's face at length. All Izumi could do was wait blankly for Nobuko's next words. After a sip of water, she continued.

'I would have moved in right away, except for my job. It's not an impossible distance to commute from Tokyo, but it meant nearly two hours on the train, and that's not to be taken lightly after all. I couldn't see any point in leaving first thing in the morning and getting home at night just in time for bed. With only Saturdays and Sundays to ourselves. He certainly isn't the type to be good-humoured under those conditions or look after things himself until I got home, and so it wouldn't have worked unless I changed my job. And he'd known that all along . . .

'I was in a quandary. It wasn't a job I could afford to throw away, and I couldn't count on finding one as good here. That was what I told him: that in any case I couldn't manage it right away. He understood and assured me he'd wait patiently. "Things aren't always as straightforward as they might look, are they?" he said.

'So I said, "Well, at least I'll spend the weekends here from now on. That way I'll be able to make a few contacts and hunt for a new job." . . . There was never any question of living with him as husband and wife in the usual sense, and being supported by him. He's timid, and extremely jealous, and since he knows his failings only too well he's put the thought of a wife and children out of his mind. And I can't do exactly as I please either. I have my family in the country to think of. Sending them money is the least I can do, and I've always kept it up.

' . . . So then he said, "That's not a bad idea, but when it doesn't suit me I'll tell you." I answered, "Oh, that's all right, I won't mind if you aren't there" – because I was still thinking only of myself at that point. "There's plenty to keep me busy," I said, "laundry and tidying up and so on." . . . Deep down, it seems, he was disappointed in me. He must have said to himself, "Huh, is that all she can think about?" I suppose I should have demanded to know at once why it wouldn't suit him and what he was doing, but if I *had* asked he might have decided he couldn't stand my jealousy. Or if I'd innocently said, "I know how busy you are," he'd have accused me of acting the proper little miss . . .

'What he did say, though, with a funny expression on his face, was "Would you like me to get an extra key made?" I said fine, though I had a feeling something was wrong. And he said, "I won't be out, and I won't be alone either. You can do the washing if you like, but I'll be getting it on with someone I'll be bringing back here." Well, of course, that made me furious. I asked him, "If you've got someone else, how could you invite me to live with you again?" He put it this way: "It can't be helped. As far as she's concerned, we're doing all right." '

Nobuko's order of pizza and Izumi's spaghetti arrived. Izumi began eating alone, nodding from time to time as Nobuko went on.

'I think he may have been in a spot himself. I believe he may really have wanted to be more intimate with you as well, Izumi. I know he enjoyed talking to you. You're from that part of Tokyo, aren't you? He's told me a little about you. Knowing you seems to have taken a weight off his mind. You'd think he'd have forgotten about me, but his mind doesn't work that way. He gets himself into strange tangles instead. He started playing tricks on you, too, didn't he? . . . He did the same to me. That is, I don't know if the tricks were the same, but . . . It's one of his peculiar theories that people don't take things in when they're merely told. So he seems to have convinced himself that we had to be made aware of this three-way arrangement by the most concrete means he could think of . . . I won't go into the details of what he did to me, but I can tell you I had a very rough time, too. I expect that neither of us came off any better than the other, you know . . .

'Then I heard you were keeping away from him and, well, you know how he is, I'm sure it's been a blow to him though he won't admit it. But frankly I felt that unless I met you myself I'd be leaving a gap, an area that I could never be sure about . . . Also, he wanted us to meet and talk, and even if I never hear another word about you there are sure to be times when I'll think of you, and the picture will be clearer in my mind if I've got an idea of what you look like, you see . . . Izumi, what do you make of jealousy? I've got jealousy on the brain – he's had that effect on me . . . '

Caught unprepared by Nobuko's question, Izumi took a moment to collect her thoughts. It was true, Takashi had certainly gone on about jealousy.

'Well . . . the usual answer is possessiveness, isn't it? But it strikes me that's not quite it . . . Could it be pride? A state where no matter what you do you can't have confidence in yourself – that might be more like it.'

'I'm not sure either . . . There was something he once said: women

70

want you to be jealous, that's all they ever think about. He accepts jealousy in that sense as perfectly natural, and yet doesn't believe he'd be capable of it himself. He says the very idea is ridiculous . . . One time I asked him why he went to all the trouble of seeing another woman when he must be finding it a drag, and he said he sometimes had to remind me of my own capacity for jealousy. He goes through life dreading his own jealous nature, so that as soon as he finds a relationship that takes some of the pressure off – as I did, and you did – he can't rest until he's satisfied himself that the other person is jealous too. And while he's at it he seems to lose his own balance. It's both a disappointment and a relief when it turns out that we are jealous, and then he starts brooding over what makes us that way, which leads him into very deep water . . .

'I don't pretend to understand much about it, but it seems something happened in his early teens. I don't know how significant it might be . . . When I'd just started living with him, we went out for a drink with a man he'd been to school with in Tokyo – in your part of town. The man had some business near his office and called in to invite him to a class reunion at his junior high. I suppose the novelty of living with me hadn't worn off then, and he was in a good mood . . . Well, we went out together and he chatted about me and where we were living, and they reminisced, and then at some point their conversation went like this: "Come to the reunion!" "Not on your life!" Then the other man said, "It's all right, you-know-who is in the States, and won't give a damn about what happened all those years ago, anyway." When he heard that he turned pale and knocked the man over, sending his chair crashing, then walked out and left him lying there. The next day he still looked so fierce I didn't like to ask what had happened with "you-know-who".

'Quite a time later – it would have been about four months after that – his mother came to see how we were getting on. He wasn't in at the time and she only stayed half an hour, but she brought up the same subject.

'She told me that when he was at junior high a girl in his class had transferred to another school after attempting suicide. If it hadn't been for that unfortunate business, she said, he'd have gone on to a good university and a job in Tokyo. "But I suppose he's standing on

71

his own feet," she said, "and I can't ask better than that." I wanted to know more about the "business" at his school, because it had me worried by this time. And his own mother admitted she couldn't make head nor tail of it.

'The girl who attempted suicide had sent him a postcard. The writing was so big it jumped right out at you, she said, and without meaning to she read it. "My life is not worth living and it's your fault. I'll come back and curse you to your death." The family was stunned. They couldn't get any explanation out of him. They hoped it might be some sort of chain letter, since kids of that age are still children when you get down to it. But his mother was worried enough to go to his school and make inquiries.

'She learned the girl had tried to gas herself but was saved and afterwards sent to another school. This really horrified his mother. She told his teacher about the postcard and asked, "Was my boy the cause?" The teacher answered flatly that he couldn't have been. He said that according to one of the boys who'd been friendly with the girl, as well as her family's account, she'd been troubled about bad grades. When his mother pointed out the postcard the teacher could only say, "Well, Takashi is one of our top students. Perhaps she had a grudge."

'His mother later got hold of some of his classmates and managed indirectly to find out about his connection with the girl who'd changed schools. The story seemed reassuring. It was actually the girl's boyfriend he'd been friendly with from the start, and he'd had nothing to do with the girl. All the same, when he came to take entrance exams for senior high he balked at going to the local high school, but she didn't give this much thought because his reason was that he wanted to go to a more challenging school. Then he chose a college even further away and left home, which started her thinking that perhaps she *had* seen some sort of change come over him after what had happened. Not that she could have asked him about it, though. It had been too long ago, she said, and he wouldn't have told her the truth . . . What do you think, Izumi?'

Izumi had long since finished her spaghetti. The untouched pizza in front of Nobuko had gone hard and flat.

'Hm . . . I'm not sure there's much sense in wondering about such things. It happened at junior high, after all. What's more to the point right now – aren't you going to eat that? We'd better be moving on pretty soon . . . '

Nobuko looked hastily around. No other customers remained.

'Oh, are they closing? It's all right, I don't need to eat. Shall we go? Actually, I was awfully hungry before meeting you, and so I stopped at the noodle stand in the station.'

They stood up and, paying their separate bills at the counter, headed for the trains. As they walked, Nobuko said in a low voice:

'But . . . even a child – a baby – can be terribly jealous. Haven't you heard stories about a toddler who kills a baby brother or sister out of jealousy? How would the child live with that when it grew up, I wonder? The parents might pretend on the surface to have forgotten, but surely their ties with the child would be affected somehow. I can't even imagine it, myself . . . I was jealous of my older sister, though, and of the teacher's pet, and in my own small way I know those things can surface again years later, when you least expect it . . . Haven't you ever felt anything like that?'

Izumi couldn't answer at once, and before she did they came to the subway entrance, where Nobuko said simply, 'Well, this is my station.' As Izumi automatically gave a slight bow of her head, Nobuko put on a smile and went bouncily down the stairs. She didn't glance back though Izumi waited, so with a sigh Izumi started walking. At the back of her mind were the dim figures of three thirteen-year-olds: Takashi and the other boy had their arms round each other's shoulders, while on the opposite side the boy held hands with the girl as they looked happily into each other's faces.

'If you've got a few minutes,' Kazuko had requested, 'would you mind coming over? I'm going to give the place a cleaning now that the weather's warmer, but I don't like the thought of taking that cover off the fluorescent light by myself, so can I get you to do it for me?'

'What's so frightening about dead insects?' Amused at Kazuko's cowardice, Izumi had come out in jeans and a sweat shirt. It was early in April. Even the light drizzle that fell from time to time seemed to add freshness to the spring mood in the air, and when the sun shone she half closed her eyes in rapture, wanting to spread her arms, to open and spread her body too. Pale cherry blossom petals were sticking to the curb and the roofs of parked cars. The cherry trees in the park in front of Kazuko's building, having just passed the season's peak, were showering their blossoms as lavishly as she'd expected.

'I came over because I knew you'd turn on a great view,' Izumi told Kazuko from the balcony as she enjoyed the sweep of flowering cherries that filled her mind with their haze. 'I wouldn't worry about a few insects if a fringe benefit like this came with them.'

Kazuko's daughter was sitting on the floor, her eyes eagerly following first Izumi then her mother.

'I know, but the season is over so quickly. After the blossoms have fallen we get a shower of caterpillars instead.'

To Kazuko's offer of tea, Izumi said she'd get the job done first and pulled out a dining chair, positioned it under the light, and stepped up. Her raised arms easily reached the ceiling. As she set about groping with both hands around the edges of the plastic cover, she marvelled at how the builders of apartments economised on ceiling height.

'How are you doing? Think you'll need a screwdriver?' Kazuko, like her daughter at her side, was gazing up.

'No, I don't think so.'

Izumi tried gently rocking the cover back and forth.

With dismaying effortlessness it slipped from the frame. The cover itself was a flimsy thing that changed shape at the slightest pressure of her fingertips.

'Well, will you look at that? It was only clipped on.' Izumi stepped down holding it in both hands. 'What a letdown. Feel it – you'd never have guessed it was a piece of cheap plastic, would you?'

'It's full of dead insects! Let me see!' said Kazuko's daughter gleefully as she peered into the cover.

'No, no, quick, throw them out. The trash bag's over there.' Kazuko's frown of distaste made Izumi want to tease her. She said to the little girl:

'Oh, there's nothing wrong with taking a peek, is there? It'll help you in nature study, won't it?'

'Mm! Let me see! Let me see!'

Izumi hurriedly set the cover down on the floor before the child's tugging could spill the contents.

74

'Oh, don't! For a girl, she's awfully keen on insects.'

'That's not a bad thing. They're all tiny, anyhow. I can't see any harm in it.'

While Izumi and Kazuko wrangled, the girl was already investigating the dead insects one by one with her right hand. Over her shoulder Izumi spied green ones, black ones, little moths, winged ants, mosquitoes – such an accumulation of bodies that if she were to start counting she'd be at it for a couple of hours.

'Oh, no, don't touch them. What a dirty child you are.' Kazuko gripped her daughter's arm and spoke in genuine irritation.

Since there was no need to side with the little girl to the point of quarrelling with Kazuko, Izumi suggested, 'Well, your mother says that's enough, so let's finish with them now, shall we?' and put her hand on the cover.

'Are you going to throw them away? All of them?' the girl demanded resentfully of Kazuko.

'Of course. We'll throw them out and wash it nice and clean.'

'Let me have just one. Just one! There was a really strange one. Please, please can I?'

Unable to stand by, Izumi held the case out to the girl and said to Kazuko, 'She can have *one*, can't she?'

Kazuko nodded sourly. Seeing this, her daughter gave a beaming smile and pored over the cover's contents. Immediately she picked a black insect and thrust it in Izumi's face. 'This one!' Izumi had no choice but to take the insect on the palm of her hand.

'Let's see.' It was not a particularly rare species by the look of it: just a beetle with a white pattern in the centre.

'This one?' Izumi couldn't help inquiring. The girl nodded with complete assurance.

'That's right. There's a picture on it of a person with their arms tied behind their back. They're going the other way.'

'Going the other way?' In surprise, Izumi took a closer look at the insect's wings. Though it was a minute pattern on a tiny insect less than half an inch long, once she put it like that it did seem not unlike a human form. Izumi wouldn't have said it was walking away, though. Rather, it suggested a forlorn figure poised for an instant before plunging into deep darkness.

75

'Want a look?' Izumi asked Kazuko.

'No, thanks! It gives me the creeps . . . If you want to keep it, wrap it in a piece of paper,' Kazuko said briskly, and signalled Izumi with her eyes to hurry and dump the insects out of the cover.

Two days later Kazuko phoned about the insect. When her daughter's father came to stay the night before, the girl had wanted to show him her 'treasure'. But the insect had vanished from its tissue wrapping. In consternation the girl had searched the room, but without success. 'It can't be helped. Maybe it came to life and flew away,' the father suggested to his sobbing daughter. 'Tell me about it. What kind of insect was it?' The girl described it. With a look of extreme surprise, her father muttered, 'Sounds like a *kikumushi*.'

'Is that what it's called?' the girl asked. 'Chrysanthemum beetle?'

'It might have been. But if so then it really is rare, and when it's dis-covered it turns into a white butterfly and flies away.' The daughter breathed a sigh of relief at this explanation: so it had turned into a butterfly and flown away.

Once the girl was in bed Kazuko had chuckled, 'Not bad for an ad-lib.'

At which he'd shaken his head seriously and answered, 'I wasn't making it up, I heard it ages ago when I was a child. It was the kind of gruesome thing I wished I hadn't heard. You know the Okiku [Chry-santhemum] of ghost-story fame, the one from the Manor of the Dishes? She was a servant in a samurai household, and the master was in love with her. In a fit of jealousy his wife hid a needle in her hus-band's food and claimed it was Okiku's doing. This brought down the master's wrath on Okiku's head, and she was shoved down an old well with her hands tied behind her back. Then her mother threw her-self down the well after her. Ever since – and it was hundreds of years ago – Okiku's longing for vengeance has lived on in the form of an insect. They say that on its back the insect has a likeness of Okiku, seen from behind, as she's about to be pushed down the well. And that after the *kikumushi* has lived a certain length of time it changes into a butterfly and flies up to heaven.'

'She says she can't believe it was really such a remarkable insect,' Izumi told Takashi, 'but the thought of it woke her up in the night with the shivers. I wonder. I saw it too. The pattern wasn't obvious at first sight, but it certainly could have been a person falling into a well.'

Nothing had changed in Takashi's room. The green of the trees loomed just outside the open window, as in Kazuko's apartment. In the dark of night the young leaves floated as palely and hazily as blossoms.

'Don't you get a lot of insects in here, too? If you kept an eye out for it you might find a chrysanthemum beetle.'

Takashi glanced at the young leaves showing at the window. '... But let's face it,' he said, 'having the insect turn to a butterfly and take off to heaven is a bit far-fetched.'

'Mm. But otherwise Okiku's malice would live for ever, and the story wouldn't sit right. It would have been too powerful, don't you think?'

'Because the insect is still with us.'

'That's right. I saw it, in fact. I wonder what its proper name is?'

Takashi rolled over in bed and lay on his stomach. Izumi turned into the same position and glanced at the lobe of Takashi's ear. It was tinged with a colour that seemed too beautiful for a man's.

'There really was a woman called Okiku, wasn't there?' he said. 'The story became famous overnight when the mother threw herself down the well in protest at her death. The mother's virtuous deed was so widely admired, the role of tragic heroine was ready-made for Okiku.'

'Since even you and I know the story today, you'd think her soul would be able to rest in peace.'

'You'd think so, wouldn't you?' Takashi laughed a little. '... But if Okiku really existed, I wonder what became of the jealous wife who must have existed too?'

'After the truth got out she was probably investigated, but she hadn't committed murder directly . . . I don't know. In those days, maybe she'd have had to kill herself, and they'd have told her to get on with it.'

'I guess the husband would be beheaded, since he was the direct culprit. But when you think about it, wouldn't the wife's spirit have more reason than Okiku's to come back from the grave? It all started with her husband falling for a maid, which was mortifying enough, but she didn't have the right to dismiss her. So she'd have tried to drive her out. But maybe Okiku wasn't a very sensitive girl. If she had been, you'd think she'd have found some way of getting round the wife, getting into her good books. Or maybe, knowing the master loved her, Okiku let it go to her head. Anyway, the wife's bitterness escalates till she puts a needle in the husband's dinner. It would never have killed him. It was surely no more than a silly piece of mischief. But the husband flies into a rage and has Okiku killed – though his wife may have encouraged that – and then even Okiku's mother throws herself accusingly down the same well. They can't hush it up any longer, and the wife finally has to commit suicide. The husband curses her on the way to his execution. It must have been a nightmare for her from beginning to end. And all because her husband couldn't keep his hands off the servants. There'd be no rest for her soul. What comfort could there be for a grievance like that? So her ghost still comes out at night. You know, I begin to feel sorry for her, somehow . . .'

'No one knows what really happened. And her story and Okiku's aren't the same – class would have entered into it, too. No, you can say what you like but Okiku's the heroine,' Takashi said, watching Izumi's face.

Izumi nodded. 'And anybody will tell you that Okiku was a beauty, and the jealous wife was ugly . . . No, you're right, I suppose. The story of the jealous wife doesn't give people a thrill. With a woman like Okiku, now, in a position of weakness, the plaything of destiny bewailing her fate as she goes to a tragic death – a woman like that doesn't actually mean much to us, so we can afford to be fascinated by her and think "how lovely". How lovely it must feel to inspire such jealousy. I'm sure that's why Okiku's story has become so famous. We can forget ourselves and share just a little of Okiku's pleasure . . . That's not such a bad thing, you know, because meanwhile we're spared being jealous of anybody at all.'

Takashi had his arms one on top of the other and was resting his cheek against them. Wanting to feel the cool breeze blowing in, Izumi sat up and gazed toward the window.

' . . . That's how I feel, you know,' she added. 'I couldn't possibly be lying here with you if I didn't have such dreams . . . Neither could you . . . ' Takashi didn't answer.

' . . . But we won't allow Okiku eyes and a mouth like ours. Or arms that she could move freely. If she so much as opened her mouth or took a look out of her eyes we'd want to beat the daylights out of her – the shameless hussy. We're as jealous as that. And Okiku's ghost knows it, so all she ever shows is her back view as she falls into the old well . . . Perhaps her spirit still roams not because she can't rest but because we won't let her. For a woman as enviable as Okiku, wanting paradise would be too greedy altogether . . . You're the opposite, you know. Nobody would be fascinated by you, so you could probably go straight to paradise . . . Though I don't know you very well yet. Really, you're full of things I don't know yet.'

Something small and white came fluttering in the window, carried on the breeze. Wide-eyed, Izumi held her breath. It fell onto the grey rug. Izumi persuaded herself to get out of bed and go slowly over to it. It wasn't anything that moved. She bent down, naked, and timidly took a closer look. It was a soft young leaf about an inch long. Laughing to herself, Izumi picked the leaf up. She was going to say something to Takashi, but he was lying still on his stomach with his face in his arms as if he hadn't noticed her move. She couldn't believe he'd dropped off to sleep but she checked herself and, returning to the bed, sat down by his feet. It was nearly time to go back to her mother's. She was thankful that it wasn't too hard to go outside at this season of the year.

She glanced at Takashi's head. His stiff hair was lightly wavy. She pictured scores of tiny black insects turning one by one to white butterflies and wavering into the air. Was Takashi conjuring up the same scene and watching enraptured? Izumi stood up distractedly.

Each of the chrysanthemum beetles is Takashi, and when its body becomes vaguely restive and itchy it begins gradually changing shape, growing softer, till it exhales deeply and wafts upward like a petal. Hey, he says, exhilarated, this feels great! The same thing is happening over here, and there too. And every one of them is Takashi himself. Glancing around he sees a great many fluttering white butterflies, like a shower of blossoms. I thought I was in big trouble when I first turned into an insect, but if this is what happens it's not so bad, Takashi thinks with a blissful smile. Though now that his body is a butterfly's, being lighter, it works differently from a black beetle's and he can't move the way he wants at all. Wafting gently on the breeze is comfortable, though he supposes it's an uncertain kind of comfort . . .

Takashi sat up and looked at her. Izumi smiled, with a touch of embarrassment.

M I S S I N G

After more than half an hour standing bemused under the light, the mother firmly flipped the switch. At once the brightness of the mercury-vapour streetlamps and neon signs outside surged in through the glass as if barely able to hold back till the room was dark. Alarmed, the mother hurriedly flicked the switch on again and restored about herself the narrow ring of light to which her eyes were accustomed, while beyond the window the proper darkness of night returned. The mother gazed around her daughter's room, which she had just cleaned an hour ago; no matter how many times she looked it remained too neat. Bending towards the window she peered at the wooden fence half-hidden by shrubs, then, having first taken a deep breath, she turned the switch off once more and sat down like a deflated balloon.

For some time the mother listened tensely for any stirrings outside. The only sounds that reached her ears, however, were those of cars speeding like ambulances down the main street, the violent din of road works, and the muffled barking of what must be an old dog.

When she tired of straining her whole body in expectation of something – the click of heels on the paving, perhaps – the mother leaned forward and with the nail of her little finger painstakingly picked out scraps of rubbish wedged deep in the crevices between the tatami mats on which she was sitting. There were all sorts of oddments: the seed of a summer tangerine, pencil shavings, hairs, a nail paring, cracker crumbs, lint, an unidentifiable black pellet (possibly the breath freshener Jintan) . . . She set the scraps, one by one, in a row along the border of the tatami. Odd that they hadn't caught her eye while the room was light. She'd swept so thoroughly, too. Now she'd have to get the vacuum cleaner and give it another going-over.

Picking up a bit of sky-blue thread and placing it on the palm of her hand, the mother sighed. One person's daily round had thrown up this much debris from somewhere – though the girl had had this room next to the entrance hall to herself for only five years. The mother's hand, pale in the light from outside, was shaking like a withered leaf in the wind. Seeing the distinct shadow it cast on the tatami, she was again surprised at how bright it was out there.

The last train must have returned to the depot hours ago. She didn't need to see a clock, she could tell by the ache at the back of her eyes. Already more than eight hours – one-third of a day – had elapsed since she'd come home. By this time she would normally be so sound asleep that cats and dogs could brawl beside her pillow and she wouldn't know it. This thought helped to make up for the two big yawns she'd let out, one right after the other, an hour or so earlier. She wasn't used to this business of staying up all night – not like her girl. Children these days (children who insisted they weren't children any more) seemed to make a habit of it.

After yawning in spite of herself the mother had none the less felt both shame and weariness. And she began to be bothered by the glow of the electric bulb whose reddish tinge seemed to lure and compel her towards sleep. Whatever happened, she mustn't sleep on a night when she didn't know where her daughter was. That was what parenthood meant.

Before she did her daughter's room, the mother had cleaned the house from top to bottom. She had polished the kitchen floor and washed every window in sight. She had laundered the curtains and sheets, though she hadn't hung them out in the yard – they were still in the spin dryer. She'd never believed in drying the washing at night, as she'd heard the children wouldn't stop wetting their beds if she did. But hadn't the laundry and the housecleaning made far too much noise for the middle of the night? Remembering, the mother blushed. Wouldn't the neighbours have noticed? Besides, what if her daughter had come home and caught her busily wiping windowpanes? How she'd have laughed – she was such a tease. 'At this hour? What's the matter? Been having nightmares? And why are you still wearing black? . . . '

Her daughter's imagined inquiry startled her. It was true, she hadn't as much as taken off her formal white socks since arriving home from the memorial service. She hadn't omitted to make dinner, and close the shutters, and even neatly shine several pairs of shoes that her daughter had left, and yet she'd overlooked her own costume like some absent-minded child forgetting her schoolbag – as her daughter had twice done in second grade. The sleeve of her black kimono was, she saw, already speckled with dust. But the mother didn't feel like changing her clothes. Not unless she could change into her nightdress.

She must be more tired than she realised, thought the mother as she straightened the dishevelled neckline of her kimono. She had been on the move since early morning, travelling to a seaside town two hours distant where the seventh anniversary service was to be held in memory of her sister; it was the longest trip she'd made in years. On reaching the temple she was at once ushered through to the back, where her aunt asked her to prepare tea and cakes for thirty people. There were two girls as helpers, but they were more useless than her own daughter. (She gathered they were the daughters of the eldest son of the family into which her late sister had married, but didn't recall having seen them before.) And what's more they appeared to have taken the memorial service for some kind of party, for whenever they spotted an unknown boy of their own age among the distant relatives they whispered together with stifled mirth.

Her own daughter had surely learned only too well, through the mother herself, what worthless creatures men were. A man was the sort who'd sire any number of children and then run off when the mood took him (when a young woman gave him a suggestive smile). The sort who was capable of amusing himself with some young floozy while his wife washed diapers. And then anonymously sending senseless expensive toys. At times, though, the mother would fall to wondering whether it was not so much that men were worthless, but that the women attracted to the fellows were fools. At her son's wedding three years ago she'd looked over the bride, who was even plainer than her daughter, with mixed feelings. But never

82

mind her son, it was her daughter she needed to watch over. In bringing her up the mother had taken pains to speak ill of the husband who had deserted them and of men in general. Thanks to her efforts, her daughter hadn't yet made a single male friend. At least, not as far as she knew. For the time being the mother was satisfied. Her mind was made up: she must never allow her to follow in her own footsteps.

Had her daughter been packing her bags in this room about the time the mother was thinking these thoughts in the seaside town? What expression could she have been wearing? A pout and a frown? Or was she in tears? No, that she couldn't imagine: why leave home if it made her cry? She must have set out as if going on nothing more than a hiking trip. But who with? It was unthinkable that her daughter, who'd been minding the house, would simply go off of her own accord.

In the temple hall, seated opposite her brother-in-law, who'd remarried, and the children, the mother had let her attention stray from the reading of the sutras to memories of her sister, dead of cancer after a brief six months' stay in the hospital. In their schooldays the mother, who was the younger of the two, had enjoyed being shown the notes her sister often received from younger girls. Her sister liked to detect errors in their spelling and grammar. She wanted to be a language teacher or a reporter for a women's magazine. The mother felt a growing pity for the sister who'd only succeeded in becoming the parent of three grubby children before she died; the pity was stronger than it had been seven years ago, and coming on top of the memory of her own marriage it brought tears to her eyes. As for the bereaved husband, before the seventh anniversary he'd gotten himself a young wife from somewhere, impregnated her without delay, and was the picture of fond contentment. The mother had headed for home in a gloomy frame of mind, further convinced that women were the losers every time.

As she slipped off her lacquered wooden sandals in the hallway she'd called to her daughter, eager for a sight of the girl who had, after all, led a quiet life so far. She called loudly four or five times, but her daughter, who was supposed to be looking after things on her own, didn't answer. Disgruntled, the mother went into the living room. What a neglectful girl she was. A newspaper, a cup, and a bottle of digestive medicine were still on the low table where they'd been that morning; there too was the extra big round cushion that went by an English-sounding name, 'floor cushion' or some such thing, which the daughter had bought for herself – but not the daughter. She took a look in the kitchen, in the daughter's room, in her own bedroom, and upstairs in what had been her husband's preserve. The girl wasn't anywhere.

Back in the living room the mother pondered for a while, then went slowly and deliberately to the hallway and opened the shoe cupboard. On the two shelves reserved for her daughter's use there was an empty space between the boxes holding her old school shoes and her galoshes. At least three pairs were missing. Among them would be the black patent leather shoes she had bought only last month. Picking up the white sandals her daughter had kicked off at the entrance and placing them neatly alongside her own, she returned once more to the living room, where she clenched the hand whose minute trembling she had only just noticed and pressed it to her teeth.

For the next ten minutes the mother bit her hand.

'To go off to the cinema like that and not even lock up!'

Having taken her hand from her mouth to snap these words at her daughter's floor cushion, the mother was so unnerved by the loudness of her voice that she sat down beside the table. Then she clumsily opened the morning paper, which she hadn't had time to read. She was remembering her daughter's tearful face when, at fourteen, she wasn't allowed to see a film with a friend. The mother couldn't understand why she would want to go out specially to a cinema when there was the television, and furthermore, she was proposing to go with a mysterious friend whose name the mother had never even heard. Of course the mother, who could only associate cinemas with darkness, hadn't given permission. With tears forming in her eyes the daughter had submitted and apologised. She may very well have gone in secret all the same. Mothers could be fooled in any number of ways . . .

Suddenly turning pale, the mother threw the newspaper aside and rushed to the daughter's room. She surveyed it slowly, calling to mind how it had appeared before. Since she didn't look in every day – the daughter always propped the door shut from inside – her memory was vague, but she could tell that an assortment of items had disappeared. The red alarm clock the girl had treasured as a graduation present from a friend, the contents of the letter holder, the pennant from the design school she'd been attending since the spring, a large ruler, bottles of toilet water, a hairbrush, several photograph albums dating back to childhood, a black patent leather handbag that matched the shoes, the cloth shoulder bag she'd used since high school . . . The portable stereo and stack of records bought with her wages from a part-time job must have proved too bulky; these she'd had to do without. Drums and trumpets would often blare from the daughter's room in the middle of the night.

With a groan the mother sat down heavily beside the stereo. She couldn't bring herself to open the closet. It was enough that the hairbrush and the photograph albums were gone. She'd been careless in spite of having feared this very thing. Why, oh why, did children choose to imitate only their parents' folly? The frustration, slow in rising, came welling up now.

Slipping her trembling hand into the breast of her kimono, she began to examine the three black faces pictured on the jacket of one of her daughter's records. The three faces were three different shades of black: one was near indigo, one was dark brown, one verged on a deep green. Were black people's skin colours each so different? Which did they like best themselves? The mother deliberated as earnestly as she did when unable to decide the menu for the evening meal. Every time there was a sound outside the window (car horns, a drunk singing), the mother abused her unseen daughter, her face twisting. Fancy not even being capable of minding the house properly! And playing at running off, just like your father's tomfoolery . . .

A premonition had made her shiver many times before now. When her daughter was supposedly at kindergarten she'd been picked up by the police way over by the breakwater. While at grade school she'd once locked herself in the garden shed, from the inside, and stayed in hiding the whole day. The mother had asked more and more urgently what was the matter, but could get no answer but crying. And then – was it around the end of high school? – without warning the girl had come home intoxicated one night, after eleven o'clock. The mother

85

had given her a lecture that lasted fully an hour, to which the daughter had responded coolly, 'You don't have to make such a dreadful scene. I'm home now, so why all the fuss?' Beside herself with rage, the mother had grabbed at the girl, who'd stuck out a hand and quite effortlessly pushed her over, then lurched into her room. Bacteria, that's what does it, muttered the mother, and she gripped her right breast with the hand she'd tucked into the front of her kimono. Clearly, bacteria which would poison her whole system in an unguarded moment had taken hold in the girl's body – caught from her father, of course.

The mother remained seated for perhaps an hour or more. Then, leaping up as though someone had thundered in her ear, she rushed into the kitchen and began washing rice and vegetables for dinner. By the time she realised what she was doing she'd prepared quantities that would take the two of them a good three days to eat. As soon as she had carried the meal to the table and covered it with a cloth, she set to work polishing the kitchen floor. Next came the bench, then the dresser. Halfway through this another idea struck her and she took down the living-room curtains and piled them into the washing machine. While she was doing that her eye fell on the stained tiles of the bathroom wall, and she went at them with a scrubbing brush. No sooner was one thing done than the dirt in some other place assailed her. As if dodging this way and that in the path of whatever was bearing down on her, the mother darted about the house with her rags and broom. Although the lights were on she might as well have been cleaning in the dark.

The last room she did was her daughter's. This was the only one with a window on the west side of the house; as it faced onto the alley, one could keep watch on anyone who opened the gate and came to the door. While she was busily cleaning, the mother's attention was gradually drawn to the window and what might be outside. She had a notion the daughter was lurking behind the fence; she'd have made it as far as the gate hours earlier, but finding the house lit up she'd be hiding, watching her mother's movements. Wasn't she stuck in the alley, biting her lower lip and thinking, 'All I did was join a friend at the movies, and here's Mother in a fit, tearing my room apart. Anyone would think I'd run away from home.' Once this thought struck her she was unable to move a finger, clutching her broom . . .

But where *could* she be at this time of night? Rubbing her aching eyes, the mother posed the question to the bits and pieces she'd lined up along the edge of the tatami.

Over the row of scraps a scene gradually took shape: the figure of her daughter in some entertainment district bouncing like a puppy along a pavement illuminated by colourful neon signs and strings of fairy lights. No doubt she's just come out of a cinema or café. A young man the mother has never set eyes on is chatting with her, one arm encircling her shoulders. He has long permed hair, rimless dark glasses, and clothes fringed like an American Indian's. The daughter is wearing baggy red and black slacks that the mother doesn't recognise, and she too has on dark glasses.

Everything in sight is lit up like a Christmas display in a toyshop window. Even the night sky scintillates like silver lamé. Music mingles with the city's noise, and jingling sleigh bells ring in Santa Claus. Laughing (whenever her eyes meet the youth's) as innocently as when a child, the daughter is singing a song. Probably black music – not a Negro spiritual, but that soul rock or whatever it is . . .

People throng the pavements. Red faces, blue faces, yellow faces, all laughing with mouths wide open. Everybody in the district is undoubtedly drunk. The bacteria known as alcohol hang in the air like dust clouds. Therefore the daughter and her companion – who *is* that young man? – must also be drunk. Seen from behind they appear to be doing a folk dance. In the streets people lie flat on their backs, huddle over, leap into the air. How can her daughter bear the place, how can she not get dizzy? She's just a child; perhaps her head is filled with the novelty of it.

The daughter and the young man come to a stop in front of a great box of red glass. He gives her a push and they go in. A good-natured, gullible girl like her can't turn anyone down. The red glass box is packed with jostling Santa Clauses. Reindeer, too, with tumblers of whiskey in hand. Glass beads snow from the ceiling, glinting every colour of the rainbow. In the midst of the snowstorm, swinging on a trapeze, are dwarves who might have stepped out of a fairy tale, while beyond them a motorcycle team dives through flaming hoops. The daughter gazes enraptured at the box of bedlam. Before she knows it, the youth at her side has also donned a Santa costume.

87

A reindeer approaches and hands them each a whiskey. They drink a toast with the animal, draining their glasses dry. Whereupon the youthful Santa Claus gives some sort of order to the daughter. Laughing ticklishly she strips off her clothes, underwear and all. Then she mounts the reindeer's back. Next the young man mounts. As he's about to give the deer a flick of the whip he takes off his dark glasses and reveals his face. A face familiar from somewhere (narrow eyes like the daughter's, a flared nose): the face of her husband . . .

Instantly the mother was on her feet, shaking all over. For her husband's face, of all things, to appear – she doubted her own reason. What had come over her? Santa Clauses, and her daughter naked? Where had things gone wrong? With a brisk shake of her head, as if to throw off an animal clinging to her hair, she leaned out of the window and whispered to the fence in a quivering voice:

'. . . Are you . . . there, dear?'

There wasn't a rustle, nor, of course, an answer.

Again the mother sat down in the middle of the darkened room. She told herself to wait, not to think any more – which only gave rise to a great many more thoughts, keeping her busy brushing them off. Like a swarm of flies – she'd no sooner kill one than a new one would buzz in her face. The mother closed her eyes and blocked her ears and the other flies disappeared from view, leaving only her baby daughter. She was drawing up her stubby arms and legs and bawling till perspiration stood out on her half-bald head. With her turned-up nose and eyes aslant – her father's features – no one could have called her a pretty baby.

When she had just started school, the daughter often wanted to hear about her babyhood.

'How did I sound when I cried?'

'Exactly like a cat.'

'Did I have dimples when I smiled?'

'Dimples? Oh, no, you were like a little mouse.'

'Did I sleep in a cradle?'

'In the daytime I put you down on a cushion.'

'Did I really wear diapers?'

'I had to keep you in diapers until after your second birthday, you know.'

. . .

88

'Did everyone cuddle me?'

'Who's everyone?'

'My brother, and grandmother, and father . . . '

' . . . Only me. I was the only one who cuddled you.'

'Only you?'

'That's right. Isn't that good enough for you?'

The mother stood up, watching her shadow on the tatami as she did so, and flicked the light switch. The shadow that had extended towards the desk vanished and another formed like a cat curled at her feet. She rubbed her eyes at the returning burst of light, dealt the rubbish on the mat's edge a kick that sent it flying, and stumbled out to the hallway. In the corner where she'd forgotten them were the rags and bucket. She put the rags in the bucket and, carrying the lot outside, emptied the dirty water under the shrubbery. The rags slopped out as well. Setting the bucket down beside the two humps they made – which put her in mind of dead moles – the mother opened the gate and stepped into the alley. The telephone poles and a TV aerial on the house opposite cast oblique shadows. Softly, she began to walk.

So near dawn, it was natural that every house should be dark and quiet, yet there was one window lighted like her daughter's. It was in the new block of apartments at the end of the alley. What, the mother thought suspiciously, could they be doing up at this hour? Were they waiting for someone? In front of the house three doors down, a quoit set lay in pieces. The mother fitted the peg back on the stand and placed it carefully against the wall.

She came to the main street, where the mercury-vapour lamps shone wastefully bright, the neon signs winked gaily away with no one there to see, and cars flashed by, now black, now white, on a road which looked broader in that light than in the light of day. The unexpected brightness eased the mother's mind. She wished she'd come out sooner. Her daughter must surely be in this same bright light. Releasing a deep breath – part sigh and part yawn – the mother squatted in front of the shuttered door of the corner rice store. She couldn't miss her here. Would she come home on foot or by taxi? Because of all that luggage – how much would it amount to? – she might have to come by taxi.

Hugging her knees and resting her chin on them, the mother waited for a shadowy figure to run up to her. A figure holding a cloth bundle in each hand and wearing a rucksack: a little girl in a short skirt, or a teenager, or her husband looking gaunt and tired. The figure could have been any of these. She was no longer sure who she was waiting for.

Before long, the drowsiness she'd pressed back behind her eyes began infiltrating the mother's body, dissolving from the inside. Dreamily, she found herself playing house with her six-year-old sister. Her sister, being older, was hostess. Their fruit juice was crushed from morning glories, and the stems of foxtails did for straws. From polite conversation about the weather, the sisters moved on to gossip about the neighbours.

Their mother's voice was heard.

' . . . What are you doing?'

Her sister and the juice were gone in a flash. She faltered a reply: ' . . . Waiting.'

'What a useless little thing you are . . . '

'But . . . what else can I do?'

'Such a fool of a child. I'm disappointed in you.'

' . . . Tell me, how exciting is it to go out on the town?'

' . . . You should give it a try . . . '

By some trick the voice had turned into those of her husband and her daughter. The mother said the words over again to herself. As she murmured them, tears brimmed in her eyes.

' . . . But there's nowhere for me to enjoy myself. Not now.'

'You disappoint me, you really do. Why have my children had such bad luck, the pair of you?'

Bad luck: that was it. The mother went on saying these words over to herself. The sounds gradually worked loose, drifted distinctly into the air, and faded away in different directions.

When the sounds had gone, leaving her plumped there with her bottom on the pavement and her chin buried between her knees, the mother was so fast asleep that she wouldn't have woken at once if a policeman on the beat had hailed her or a cat licked her cheek.

THE · SHOOTING · GALLERY

The two children suddenly leaned halfway out of the window of the moving train and shrieked in turn:

'Look! Over there!'

'It's all shiny!'

'Is that the sea?'

'Watch out or you'll get your heads knocked off!' Their mother gripped the children by the scruffs of their necks, one in each hand, and deposited them back in their seats. At the sound of their shouts several other passengers in the coach had roused themselves for a look. But already low hills hid the sea, which had shown its dully gleaming back for the first time in the three hours since the train left the city.

'Hey . . . wasn't that the sea?' The older boy, the seven-year-old, grumblingly rested his chin on the window-sill and glowered at the green hills. The mother put her arm around the shoulders of his younger brother, who was four, in the seat beside hers and after a moment's hesitation answered:

'The sea . . . mm . . . Listen, we're getting off at the station after next. Put your shoes on, please, so you'll be ready.'

'The station after next?' the younger child asked with a sigh. The mother's only reply was to let her head recline against the backrest and close her eyes.

'There's something wrong. Mom, it wasn't like you said it'd be . . .'

'Ugh! My shoes are all wet with orange juice,' whimpered the younger child, who had been investigating under the seat.

'Hey, you're right. That's nothing, though. I'll make them good and wet.'

'No! Don't!'

'They'll only get wet anyway at the beach. Here, give them to me and I'll soak 'em for you.'

'Nooo! I said don't!'

'You're squealing like a girl, stupid.'

The younger child clung to his mother's arm and burst into tears. 'Mom, he hit me again. He's always *picking* on me . . . '

Their mother, her eyes firmly shut, was pretending not to hear.

The thought of the sea had come to her suddenly the night before. She had no idea why; indeed it struck her as very strange. She'd made up her mind to take the two children to the beach.

There she had been, hemmed in by the cracker crumbs, plastic blocks, empty juice cans, underwear and socks that littered the room, the sinkful of dirty dishes, the wash hanging from the ceiling, the sound of the TV, the younger child's crying, her own voice talking at the office, and the weariness – a weariness that turned her body to a desiccated old sponge. Unable to lie down, she was sitting having a cigarette with her elbows resting on the table when a transparent blue gleam streaked before her eyes. It was brilliant and cool. Like the smell of menthol. The mother chain-smoked three cigarettes, after which, feeling sick, she lay down with her face against the tatami matting. It was then that she recognised the sea. It could only be the sea. It had completely slipped her mind. She'd known something was wrong all along, though, and now it came to her: it must have been the sea that had got left out.

She eventually noticed the older boy standing just in front of her head. 'Move out of the way,' he told her, 'we want to put our beds down.'

The mother was obliged to get up. As she leaned against the wall and watched the two children carry their folded futons from the closet and efficiently lay them down, she was still thinking, 'The part that was left out – the sea, blue light, waves, all the things I'd forgotten till now . . . '

After changing into pyjamas she brought out an old bottle of whiskey and began to drink it with water.

' . . . Tomorrow we must go to the sea. Before it slips my mind again . . . '

The older child, who was studying an illustrated book of trains, twisted around and lifted his head from the pillow to stare up at his mother's face already flushed with the whiskey. The child's pale face with its firm mouth. He takes after his father. But the child doesn't know his father, nor does the father know the child now. If they don't know each other, maybe 'take after' isn't the right word. The child doesn't really take after anyone. His only commitment in life is to himself. A father who never existed. But thanks to the child the mother could never entirely forget the father – in spite of the pride she'd taken in managing to watch him go and not pursue him, nor turn her face away, though she hadn't quite risen to a smile; and in spite of the way she'd congratulated herself on her courage when, having been pregnant with the younger child at the time, eight months later she'd given birth alone.

'The sea?' The younger child stood up on his bed and asked, 'Did you say the sea?'

'Yes, I did . . . You two ought to have a chance to see the real thing too . . . '

'The sea . . . but there's school tomorrow.' The older boy sat up in bed.

'Tomorrow's Saturday. It's a half-holiday anyway . . . Take the day off.'

'But . . . why are we going? Is there something special?'

'Don't be silly,' his younger brother objected. 'It's the sea. The sea! . . . Wow, can we really go?'

' . . . What beach are we going to?'

The younger boy hugged his brother's head from behind and gave it a good shake. 'The sea! The *sea*!'

Their mother laughed.

'It's deep blue,' she said, 'and it sparkles different colours. Sometimes it glitters like gold. Maybe it'll smell like oranges – those navel oranges you like so much. And maybe we'll hear the fishies' voices coming from under the water.'

'You're kidding,' said the younger child.

'Bet you've never even been,' said the older.

The mother turned her face away. The whiskey bottle was empty. Drinking had made her hot. She caught a whiff of the sea, but it was sickeningly strong. A nasty smell. The idea of going began to scare her. She was afraid something would be taken from her, afraid of disintegrating. Maybe it wasn't the sea she'd seen after all – that transparent blue gleam just now. Then what could it be? . . . The sea. It had to be. At least, she couldn't think of anything else. Then she'd have to go. Courage. She'd go and have a look even though – no, *because* – she was scared. A silly sort of courage, but courage none the less . . .

The younger boy was pretending to swim on his bed. Soon both brothers were tumbling together. It was after eleven o'clock. The mother lay down and, since there was no more whiskey, started on the cigarettes. She tried to see the whiteness of sea spray in the smoke issuing from her mouth. It wasn't easy.

She'd grown up far from the sea herself. The view from the department store's roof or the hilltop lookout point in the park was of mountains, not the sea. Her first outing to the beach came during summer vacation when she was eight years old – a day trip with her mother to her aunt's house in a seaside town. It was not long after her father's death. The train was packed with picnickers on the way there and again on the way back. The two of them sat on sheets of newspaper they'd spread on the corridor floor in a crowded compartment. The day might as well have been an exercise in learning what exhaustion meant. As she knew more or less how to swim from lessons in the school pool, she was able to make a fair enough showing in her first encounter with the sea. Once she was over her initial wariness of the waves there was nothing to it. She had a go at the sorts of things the other kids were doing, building sandcastles and burying her mother's thin body in the sand, though not entirely sure why these were meant to be such fun. She smilingly agreed that she'd had a good time. But she hadn't really appreciated the sea that day. The sea wouldn't share any of its light or smell with a mere girl of eight.

They'd gone again two years later, and two years after that there'd been a class picnic. On each occasion the sea remained plain tepid salt water. She'd never felt any great desire to go there. In those days, she now saw, it was the surface of a swimming pool in the centre of Tokyo that had sparkled for her.

Then when had she discovered the sea? Her memory was vague on this, the most important point. Ten years ago? Five? A friend had once invited her to the coast in winter. She'd gone once by herself, and even made the ferry crossing to an island. None of these scenes was clear in her mind. In fact perhaps she, like her children, had yet to see the real thing. Conceivably, though, the sea might have filtered into her body over the years in tiny fragments like the parts of a picture puzzle which, while she'd never identified the whole, had pieced themselves together as the sea in all its sparkling radiance. An internal sea. Untouched by anyone . . .

Having drunk too much, the mother was beginning to drift off with the sound of the children's high-pitched voices in her ears.

Fragments of the sea . . . Could she trace the matrix into which she'd fitted them all the way back to the flood of light she'd experienced at the moment of birth? The light was pain. She didn't actually remember that time, of course. She'd thought she was reminded of it when she heard the first cries of her own children: yes, she'd thought then, it was painful and dazzling, and I couldn't help crying. With every cry I was longing to accustom myself to the flood of light. But before my body had time to adjust, the light had ceased to exist as light. Perhaps what I was seeing was the brightness of the internal sea? My mother's sea.

There were other memories. The tale of the Little Mermaid she'd come across in a foreign picture book. Though it would never have occurred to her to see herself in the person of the lovely little princess, she'd been haunted by the idea that perhaps she had been present herself, somewhere in the deeps where the princess lived. She sensed the sea's wan bluish gleam in the Little Mermaid's sobs.

And then eight years ago. She was walking the busy streets of the city centre with the children's father. It was early spring, a day of particularly heavy smog that was blurring the many-coloured neon lights. She'd suddenly heard waves booming. That was how she thought of it: not the sea, waves. Waves closing in. The children's father was having a fit of coughing, but insisted it wasn't a cold. What had it been, then? Was he choking on the smell of the sea too? Was

95

that what drove him to try living with me? Being invisible, the sea could materialise anywhere. Like a thick bullet-proof glass wall rising on all sides. You raised your eyes to find a smooth, sheer blue surface towering over you. Over an island like the bottom of a well. Chill and lonely. He'd been driven into the arms of something that had body warmth – was that how it had happened? But the sea inside the body is different, it's hot and intensely bright, it seethes whitely. That was the sea she wanted to see. To go back to. And if it meant disintegration, she was ready for that too . . .

That part of the coast was predictably deserted, as the swimming season hadn't started. Only two local people got off at the same stop as the mother and her children. A large sightseeing map was displayed in front of the station beside the public toilets. The paint had peeled here and there, interrupting the black lines that represented roads, but it gave a general idea of the stretch of coast. There were more white-flagged swimming areas than she could count. It was still only April, however. It was enough for the mother if they could just go down to the shore. The souvenir shops were nearly all closed too. The road was broad and dry. They turned their backs to the station.

The houses soon thinned out and gave way to a weed-covered scrap yard, a factory that made motorboat parts, a service station, while up ahead a tourist hotel reminiscent of one of the blocks in a housing development rose into view. The mother walked on in silence. The children were following behind in a surprisingly good mood, picking the flowers off weeds, peering into the ditch where a trickle of clear water flowed. When they entered the lane below the hotel the crash of waves reached their ears at last. At the same moment they caught the sea's smell. Breaking into a run, the mother emerged onto a concrete breakwater. There was the expanse of sandy shore, and there the rolling grey sea. The wind was cold and driving; it struck her a body blow. The sea's surface appeared dusted with iron powder. Dazzled by its dull light, she shaded her eyes with her right hand. There was no one on the beach. The amount of refuse was very noticeable – detergent bottles, rotting tangerines, rubber sandals, old tires, even a broken swivel chair lying on its side. The mother stepped down onto the sand. The children had fallen silent.

Strung out along the water's edge were more beer bottles, soft-drink cans, plastic bags, ice-cream containers and bits of broken crockery, all tangled in seaweed. Standing still above the tide line she gazed at the horizon which merged imperceptibly with the overcast sky. No silhouettes of islands, no boats to be seen. The mother headed along the shoreline. On her right she could see a long narrow sea wall jutting offshore, with what seemed to be a rock platform on the far side.

The older child spoke for the first time: 'Stinks, doesn't it? . . . '

The younger child continued: 'It's dirty, there's lots of dog poop.' He was right, she noticed, and the beach was tracked with pawprints as well.

'It's not like this where we're going, is it?'

The mother walked rapidly on without a backward glance.

As she'd expected, the shore on the other side of the wall was rocky. Massed black shapes glowered at one another like live creatures that had been cavorting in the surf only moments ago when they were frozen in mid-plunge. The waves smashed with a scatter of white spray. Again there was no one else in sight. The mother made her way onto the rocks. By now the children had started whispering in a dissatisfied tone behind her.

She came to a square, shallow depression. Emerald-green algae, an aquatic forest in miniature, flourished in the warm water. Crabs large and small were scuttling among its stems, and she spotted hermit crabs and sea slugs too.

Every little pocket held a gaping sea anemone.

In the deeper pools between rocks, silver schools of tiny fish skirted the red fronds as they swayed and flowed.

The mother picked her way across, holding her breath. Then she scrambled onto a great rock that overlooked the area, settled herself in a convenient hollow and lit a cigarette. The transparent blue sparkle was not to be found. And yet: the crash of the waves. The sharp smell flung up with the spray. The sea inside her, having reached its lowest ebb, seemed to be on the rise. She lay back, smoking. The sky pressed softly down. The mother closed her eyes. She told herself repeatedly she was glad to be there; though not the one she'd had in mind, it was still the sea. She could always be reborn, as long as she had the sea . . .

97

The mother smiled with closed eyes.

. . . My tiredness will go and the energy I had at twenty will return, but that's not all. My whole body – from the toenails to the insides of my ears – will turn into something new. And then . . . ah yes, one day my back will sprout a pair of lance-shaped wings which will begin to beat, my body will visibly expand, and when the metamorphosis is complete I'll be a dragon that ascends spiralling to the heavens. I'll leave everyone watching astounded on the earth below as I soar aloft, my golden scales gleaming. Refreshed. When would this be? She didn't know, but if she kept looking forward to it one day it would really happen. And when it did, everyone would finally realise that she hadn't been just some mother. Whispering in each other's ears, 'You know, she always did seem different somehow . . . '

'What're you doing? Come on, Mom, it's no fun here.'

'Mommy, I have to pee.'

'Come on, hurry up, let's go to the beach you told us about yesterday. So where is it? Is it near here?'

Instead of answering, the mother threw away the cigarette she still had in her hand.

. . . A golden dragon, yes. And here I am, always interrupted. Why is that? When all eyes ought to be on me in a breathless hush of anticipation. As it is, not a single wing dares poke through. This isn't how it was meant to be. I don't understand it. In the children's eyes right now there's no golden dragon, there's a black ant not a quarter of an inch in length. The lively youngsters cheerfully raise their feet to stamp on it. Hold it, you two, don't you recognise me? – But our Mom's huge, she's tremendous, she can carry us on her back and fly through the air. She isn't a little pipsqueak of an ant. – Take a closer look, now. That pipsqueak is your mother . . .

'Are you asleep? Don't just sit there. Come on, take us where we're going. I'm hungry.'

'Me too. I'm *star*ving.'

'Get up, stupid . . . '

. . . The wings are ready to grow at any time. One day, when the sea rises and threatens to engulf everything in its blue light, a golden dragon will appear in the sky. A male dragon. He will utter a cry. He will cry repeatedly as he circles above the boundless sea. At the sound

I'll wake where I'm lying trampled and destroyed on the bottom and float very cautiously to the surface. Suspecting another trick. How fresh and bright it is above the surface. Waves of green, blue, yellow, red. And a flash of gold. The male dragon's long whiskers brush the lobe of my ear. My body whirls into the air. I grow wings, I grow scales. I let out a cry. My voice is no longer human – nothing so bland. With the male dragon for my guide I fly off over the sea. In my true colours. The sea spreads beneath my eyes like a glassy plain. I'm reminded of glass beads I played with often as a child. I scoop them up by the handful and they sparkle undiminished. They sparkle with my gentleness. The very thing the male dragon wanted. Where's he got to? When I'm right here waiting . . . Now why's my body shrinking? At this rate I'll end up smaller than the children. Look, I'm supposed to sit tight and wait. And here I am being swept down what seems to be a muddy ditch, and everything else along with me. I'm so pitifully small, can't you two watch what you're doing? – Oh, you again! Listen, we told you, *our* Mom is a golden dragon who flies through the air. – Can't you understand? That was years ago, it's all over now, I lost it somewhere and nobody will ever find it again . . .

'Get up, you old bag, or I'll kick you.'

'Mommy, I'm hungry. I don't like this place. It's cold.'

. . . I want to sleep in peace and quiet. Something is swirling deep in my body. I never knew it had such depths. Clear water streams from my head to my chest, from there to my stomach, and then to a deep, stagnant pool that seems to lie in my pelvis. Deep enough to be the sea, but no, it's too turbid. Something is swimming in circles in the sediment. How am I supposed to sit tight? The children peer down. I wonder if they can see to the bottom of the stagnant waters? Do they expect to find the sea here of all places? . . .

'We've had enough of this, you old bag! We're freezing! Do you want us to catch cold?'

With the older child pulling her hair, the mother struggled to her feet. The sea was undulating as heavily as clay.

They left the shore in search of a restaurant for lunch. She hoped at least to let the children have some fresh fish. First they tried the tourist hotel: only guests could use the dining room, they were told, as it was the off-season. The clock at the reception desk said eleven – it was earlier than she'd thought. They went out into the empty street, which led to the square by the station. There were several cheap places to eat, but none that featured a seafood menu. The sushi restaurant was closed for the winter. The mother wouldn't admit defeat. If they followed the coastline they should very soon come to the neighbouring town, which was more likely to cater to visitors. This stretch of the coast was so well known that even the mother had heard of it, and she had known the name of the next town in connection with a certain legend since she was a child.

Turning back onto the shore, she set off briskly. Ahead she could vaguely make out a row of three white hotel-like buildings. It shouldn't take them half an hour if they walked fast. The children were tired and starting to complain. The younger one sat down heavily on the way, but seeing his mother press on he came running after her whimpering like a dove. The older child was encouraging him to keep up, then began to ask their mother forlornly if they were going to those white buildings, breaking off occasionally to throw sand at her back and yell, 'Drop dead, stupid!'

The shoreline never varied. The sea was the colour of clay. Beyond the sea wall that continued on their right they could see empty drying racks and storage sheds for nets, houses with small vegetable plots, workshops, and a school building which was very quiet – perhaps classes were in session. A single upturned rowboat had been left on the shore. Flies buzzed around a heap of vegetable scraps. A detergent-filled creek drained frothing into the sea.

They made better time than she'd expected to the first of the white hotels. It was a brand-new building, ten storeys high. A bank of tulips bloomed along the broad terrace overlooking the shore. White chairs and tables were stacked in one corner. Not a window was open. The children ran ahead to the lobby, where the mother was again refused service. They tried the second brand-new hotel next door: the dining room was closed. There was one more, its entrance flanked by rows of palm shrubs, but the mother went straight back down to the shore. Dirty water discharged from beneath the hotels meandered over the sands. The mother walked on uncertainly. She was footsore herself by now. She wanted to sit down somewhere for at least a rest,

100

but she couldn't feel comfortable there in full view of the hotels.

Before long the younger child began to sob. His older brother shied a worn-out man's shoe at the mother's back and shouted, 'His tummy hurts, you idiot!'

She turned to find them both with tear-swollen eyes.

'Really?'

Rubbing his eyes, the younger boy nodded.

'How bad is it?'

' . . . I wanna go to the toilet . . . '

'Well . . . there's nothing we can do. Why don't you go here? . . . '

'No! I'm not a dog.'

'But nobody's looking.'

'No! I've gotta go to the *toilet* . . . '

His face was the shade of the sea.

'Will you be all right? Can you make it?'

'If you don't hurry up, he'll die!'

The older child's voice was shaking. Leading the younger child by the hand, the mother climbed an alley that ran by the hotel off to the right. She shivered at the small hand's coldness. She'd intended to go into the hotel, but spotted a diner just across the street and bustled him in there and straight into the restroom. The child, who'd been biting his lip in desperation, huddled in tears over the toilet and emitted a groan. The mother waited outside the door till he got up.

By the time she had escorted him back, three large bowls of rice topped with chicken hash* had been set down on one of the tables. The older child had already started on his. Trying not to feel sick, the mother took up her chopsticks. The younger child pressed his right cheek against the table and closed his eyes without so much as a glance at his portion. His colouring was back to normal; there seemed no cause for worry.

The older child, having finished his greasy bowlful long before them, poured himself a cup of tea and gave some to his brother. Then he turned to their mother and said, 'Why bring us to a place like this? What'd you tell us all those lies for?'

*This cheap rice dish is called 'parent and child' after its main ingredients, chicken and egg.

101

'It's my first time here, too . . . '

'Liar! You were planning to go away and leave us.'

' . . . How could you think that?'

Now the older boy's colour resembled the surface of the sea. The mother pushed her barely touched meal aside and lit a cigarette. The electric clock on the wall said half past one. So they'd walked for a good two and a half hours.

'I might've known a woman wouldn't . . . '

'What . . . ?'

' . . . I've been to the beach with Dad. I can remember. He gave me a piggyback and ran along where the waves were breaking. It was a beautiful blue sea!'

The younger child said faintly, 'Did you really? Gosh, I wish I could've gone.'

'Yeah, I've just remembered. It must've been Dad. It was, wasn't it? He took me. Why isn't he here now?'

'It . . . must've been a dream . . . '

'It wasn't a dream. Liar! He took me to the real sea.'

'What about me? I want to go too . . . '

The mother stared at the goldfish bowl on the counter, in which a lone pop-eyed black carp was swimming. She'd just been reminded herself of a certain scene that had stayed forgotten for five years. The children's father and the older boy, who was just two, were standing together outside the house they were renting at the time. As the mother arrived by taxi from the station, the child (was it her imagination or was he a little tanned by the sun?) picked up a fistful of gravel from the road and flung it at her face. Two or three pebbles struck her cheek. He backed away with a frightened smile as the mother reached out to him. At the father's impatient 'Come on and get this door open', she unlocked the house. The father went in alone, carrying his travel bag. The child burst into tears and followed him inside.

That morning, she'd nerved herself to phone her in-laws' home in the country and check what train the child and his father would be on. She'd intended to go and meet them, believing that if she did so they could be reunited. And then she'd been a quarter of an hour late. Not only had she failed to provide the welcome they hadn't requested,

102

she'd succeeded in shutting them out of the house as well, since they got there before her. She could no longer bring herself even to apologise. She was convinced that the chance she'd missed had been her very last, and once she had so convinced herself, that was what, in effect, it became.

Three weeks earlier, when the father, his nerves at breaking point, had departed for the station with the child, she had gone with them despite his attempts to turn her away. It wasn't that she thought she had the right to keep their son with her simply because she was his mother – in fact she wasn't even confident that she could go on as a parent – but she was terrified of letting the child out of her sight. As the express moved off with him and his father on board the child howled like a wild animal. The mother was left behind on the platform to endure the suspicious stares of other people seeing off the train.

The father's parents, she remembered now, lived in a distant seaside town. That would be where the child had romped in the sea to his heart's content . . .

Leaving the money for the three bowls of hash on the table the mother got up, opened the frosted glass door and set out in the opposite direction from the shore. The older child raced after her.

'Wait! He can't walk yet.'

The mother stopped for the younger child to catch up, then took him on her back. The word 'enemy' crossed her mind.

'Here, let me carry this.' The older child took over her handbag.

The street was lined with a 'nude studio' in a shed, a pinball arcade, bars, shooting galleries, and other amusements. Most of the booths and shanties were boarded up and the patches of ground between them were being farmed, though the mother couldn't tell whether the green leaves on the narrow strips were crops or weeds. The road was surfaced with sand. Before she'd gone a hundred yards under the child's weight, her forehead was moist with perspiration.

'That one's open!' shouted the child on her back.

'Let's have a go!' The older boy broke into a run. A little farther down the road the mother noticed the shooting gallery they meant – its street frontage was barely six feet across. Of course there were no other customers. The man in charge was outside spreading seaweed to dry. As soon as the older boy picked up one of the toy rifles that were lying on the stand, he came around from behind and supplied a dish of corks. The mother retrieved her handbag and handed the man a coin.

'Me too.' The younger child climbed down from her back. 'I'm going to win those toffees.'

'Big deal. I'm getting the pack of cards.'

The mother handed over a second coin. Relieved of the weight on her back she felt dizzy. She turned for a look at the sea and found it was out of sight behind tiers of tin roofs. She could see seagulls on their ridges.

'Mister, can I have another go?' The older boy received a new dish and tried again to hit the cards. He merely grazed them twice, however, and the pack refused to topple. The younger boy hadn't a hope – corks were popping away in every direction. The mother handed the man another coin for each child. Her eyes met his. She studied his face for the first time: he was a thin young man with pale lips. He gave her a smile which dimpled his left cheek.

The two children returned to their efforts with yet another dish each. This round seemed just as likely to end in disappointment. The young man's smile broadened, drawing from the mother a wry grin.

'Rats. I bet it's rigged. I give up.'

The older child slammed his gun down on the counter. Before she knew what had come over her the mother had picked it up and said, 'Rigged? Surely not. Watch this.'

The young man placed a dish of corks before her. The mother hastily reached into her purse for a coin. She heard him say, 'I'll throw these in for free . . .'

She raised her head and he nodded, straightfaced. After a moment's hesitation the mother wordlessly positioned the gun. The prizes were arranged on three levels along the wall. Bubble-gum, toffees, dolls, playing cards. The top prize was evidently the cigarette lighter. Holding her breath, she fixed it in her sights.

'You'll never hit a thing.'

'You look silly . . . Forget it, you're a terrible shot.'

The finger she touched to the trigger was trembling. She couldn't steady the end of the barrel. Was the arm which supported the rifle trembling too? She'd just been giving a piggyback to a thirty-eight-pound child, that was why. The crash of waves sounded suddenly in her ears. The mother tightened her grip on the rifle. She couldn't keep the gas lighter in the sights.

'I wish you'd stop it,' said her child. 'Stupid.'

She shifted her aim from the lighter to the pack of cards. My enemy . . .

'You'll never hit it, 'cos women can't.'

'Yeah. Not a chance.'

The mother rounded on them with the rifle at her shoulder. She pointed the tip of the gun barrel first at the older child's head, then at the younger. Both recoiled with their mouths half open. Her hands shook and the barrel rose and fell, her heart raced and she breathed hard. Her own mouth dropped open. She choked on something hot at the back of her throat. The eye pressed to the sights began to mist.

'Bang, bang . . . ' The young man's voice gave her such a start that she staggered as if hit. She quickly settled the rifle back in place on her shoulder and pointed it at him. Their eyes met over the sights. He smiled again. A tear spilled from the mother's eye, blurring the young man's face. She aimed into the centre of its vague expanse. The trigger. The mother shut her eyes. Another tear fell. A shot reverberated in her dark field of vision. The next moment, the clear blue sea swelled like an inflating balloon and there was a flash of gold.

A golden dragon . . .

The children's laughter was ringing in her ears. But how, when I've just shot them? And after I've brought them all this way because I felt sorry for them – poor kids, they'd never seen the sea. Fathers . . . I'd have been happy myself to have a strong father who'd piggyback me and run along the beach. But I'm armed and vigilant now. I'm not the person I was five years ago. I'm not falling for any more tricks, no matter how tired I might be. Now I'm not just some mother. If you ask me, a father is a delicate bird, downed with a single shot . . .

Though she hadn't noticed the young man slip around from the back of the booth, when she opened her eyes he was standing at her side.

I'm not just some mother, I don't need gentleness from people, nor from the sea . . .

The mother replaced the gun on the counter and hastily contrived a smile. As he took up the gun the young man spoke:

'All right . . . now first, you've got to hold it like this.'

He motioned the mother and children to watch from behind, then confidently took aim at the gas lighter that the mother had singled out.

With the two children, the mother watched the tip of the gun barrel eagerly.

CLEARING·THE·THICKETS

The door opened and a red colour appeared. A clear, dazzling red. The young woman stared in admiration at the dress, whose wearer she knew.

In an art class once – years ago, in high school – a classmate had selected a tube from a box of oil paints and shown it to her grandly: 'This colour is produced by crushing a certain exceedingly rare species of insect and working it into a chemical base.' It was, she understood, a very expensive pigment, and although she wasn't sure whether to believe the story of its source, the squeeze of red on the palette certainly suggested an insect's body fluid. Although clear, it had a choking viscosity. A beautiful colour, there was no doubt about that. But she expected that once on canvas it would turn heavy and sombre beside the other tints. It's so rich I wouldn't know how to handle it, she had thought. She was even aware of an odour like an ant-lion fly's.

The dress was of the same red. A light material, perhaps, for its triangle of skirt billowed coolly. It had no buttons, ribbons, or other trimmings. It suited the slender wearer well.

The young woman was not surprised to see her. Though not expecting her she'd had a feeling that she'd turn up some time, and so could have been said to be waiting. It wasn't their first meeting; in fact they had even gone on a trip together, not alone of course, but with the others from the sketching class. They had all urged him to invite this woman along. And even before that trip she had met her in the man's apartment – which she herself had never visited alone, but always with a rowdy bunch. The woman had been in the sketching class too, though not a contemporary of hers. The man had chased her for three years, people said.

When the visitor appeared, the young woman was at the sink just inside the door, washing the previous night's dishes. With the thermometer at over 30°C the water from the tap felt good. She took a special pleasure in it because she could use all she wanted. In the winter, when it ran icy cold, she did as little washing-up as possible. It was the hottest time of day, but the young woman had only just got out of bed. At least she wasn't still in her pyjamas, she thought thankfully as she stared at the woman's dress.

Turning off the tap, she smiled. She wanted above all to convey friendliness. The visitor, however, faced directly ahead and took no notice. The young woman felt invisible. The woman standing at the door didn't open her mouth, or bow her head, or move a muscle. The young woman gave up the attempt to speak to her and instead pulled back the curtain at the end of the sink area and went through to the main room.

'Your escort's here,' she said to the man, who was still in bed. He was already awake, and jumped up at her call. Seeing the figure in the doorway he nodded slightly. The young woman leaned against the wall and watched the man dress with efficient movements. The other woman also looked on from the threshold, her manner unchanged. The man moved with an intensity that was invigorating to see. The young woman remembered him in the sketching classes he taught on behalf of a well-known artist. She hadn't thought of him in that setting for some time: in this room he had adapted to her own sloppy ways. Recess is over, the young woman told herself under her breath.

'Well, then . . . ' After finally putting on his socks, the man looked back at her. She stopped leaning on the wall and gave a smile.

'Goodbye.'

'Mm, goodbye.'

The man left the room with precise steps. The visitor followed immediately behind, a bright red insect sticking to his back. She hadn't given a single glance in the young woman's direction. This hadn't seemed at all forced. Her attention had simply remained elsewhere. After closing the door the young woman looked down: the lower half of her body wasn't any less substantial than usual. I wasn't invisible, then, she thought with relief, and with that sense of relief her face contorted for the first time.

She returned to the room and sat upright on the bed. The red was still swimming like viscous matter in her eyes. How would I have acted if it had been some other colour? White, say, or blue? The young woman lay down. She drew up her legs in foetal position. The bed was hot. She should have been satisfied, having managed to say goodbye with a proper smile, which was what she'd been hoping to do. And yet there was still a sensation of something missing, as if her backbone had been pulled out. She couldn't help curling up as tight as possible. She thought scornfully how adult in size her body had grown.

But could there really be a red bug of such a clear colour? She wondered what shape it was. There were all kinds of bugs. Bugs in grass thickets. Bugs on the seashore. Bugs in trees. Bugs under rocks. Bugs in the house. Grubs and weevils. Worms in the body. The worms in the body were all blind.

The young woman closed her eyes . . .

. . . The large garden was entirely overgrown with weeds.

The old bungalow was encircled by tall growth. Since the only trees that provided any shade were along the fence, the garden was fully exposed to the strong sun. At first it was so dazzling she couldn't keep her eyes open. The grass blades shimmered white as aluminum foil. She felt as if all the colouring in the external world was massing around her, pressing together into a solid black clot.

'It grows four inches a day, you know,' said her mother, 'and there's not a thing we can do. That doesn't mean to say, though, that we can just stand back and let it grow.' Over the towel that served as a headscarf, her mother had on a floppy straw hat of the kind young children wear. With her low blood pressure her mother was normally of a pale complexion, but even she was flushed, her forehead and upper lip beaded with sweat. In her right hand she dangled a short-bladed sickle.

'Honestly, we slog away day after day, and I can't tell if it's doing the least bit of good . . . '

From behind the young woman's back came the voice of her older sister, a big woman who made their mother seem quite tiny by comparison. She wore a broad-brimmed white cotton hat, and she too gripped a sickle in her hand. Sticky grass sap streaked her red cheeks. She had put on flesh about her hips and chin, and the impression she made was quite unlike the way the young woman remembered her. She was reminded of her sister's age: there were six years between them.

At a sudden rustling in the foliage beside her, she shrank back. Two children burst shrieking out of a thicket. A thin boy of about four and a girl not yet out of diapers, like a fluff of cotton candy. Both were bare to the waist and their hair was drenched with sweat. They were burned very brown. Though she knew she could only be seeing them for the first time, there was something familiar about their features, from their noses to the line of their mouths. The sight of the three grown-ups didn't stop them for a moment as they tumbled laughing back into the grassy thickets. The young woman looked at her sister: a frown furrowed her sister's brow and the next moment she shouted, 'Go and put your hats on! You'll get your heads burned!'

'It's no good telling them,' her mother laughed. Several drops of sweat fell to the ground. The young woman mopped her own forehead and joined in the mother's laughter, but only till she caught her sister's look. She bit her lip, lowered her face, and heard her sister's voice:

'Giggly as ever, I see. How dare she come back, now, in that condition?'

Her mother's low voice took over: 'At least she's come back. That's a mercy. It's not too late even now, and we could never have coped with only the two of us.'

'Don't I know it! I'm worn out. How could she have forgotten the grass and gone off to amuse herself? . . . '

'She was born that way. Yes, born that way. So it's hardly fair to blame her . . . Oh, my, this dreadful heat! It makes me dizzy just standing here.'

The young woman was staring at her own roundly bulging belly. It could have been a watermelon she was supporting in her arms – she felt neither pain nor its weight. She looked at her mother's face, then her sister's. They were glowing a dark, tumorous red. She returned her gaze to her belly and sighed. So this was why I came back? The glare from the surrounding grass grew fiercer and tears came into her eyes. It was her own body, yet she hadn't noticed a thing till she got this big. She thought she'd gone to the hospital – was that a dream, then? Not knowing she'd been dreaming, she'd thought all her worries were over. She remembered the man. She placed both hands on her stomach: she supposed it wasn't entirely a bad thing. The tears and sweat dripped together off her chin. He was a kind person.

'Well, now, how about making a start? If we don't get a move on, the grass will swallow us up.'

The mother held up a brand-new sickle before her daughter's face. The crescent of blade was filmed with rainbow-hued oil.

'Follow us and watch closely. There's nothing difficult about it.'

'Don't leave any roots, and don't miss even the tiniest weed,' her sister cautioned with a smile.

The three crouched in a row before the towering thickets. Imitating the gestures of her mother on her left and her sister on her right, the young woman set her hands busily in motion. First she grasped a bunch of grass in her left hand, then dug into the earth at its roots with her sickle, then slowly pulled it up with both hands. Once unearthed the plant was laid down on the spot. The ground was hard, and stony besides. Rooting out full-grown grass proved harder than she would have guessed. She needed to brace herself well and put her back into the work. Tugging too vigorously or too gingerly would snap the stems off at the base and force her to rake through the soil with the sickle, painstakingly picking out the roots. She was quickly left behind. Her back ached, the palm of her hand oozed blood. Her belly felt bloated, her breathing was laboured. Every so often she had to stand up for a rest. The rear views of her mother and sister waddling ahead as they skilfully pulled the grass made her think of elongated moles.

The grass thickets sweltered. The glare and the sweat streaming from her forehead made it impossible to keep her eyes wide open. Did that mean it was noon? She looked up at the sky: it was dull and clouded. Now and then the children's voices shrilled from an unexpected quarter of the garden. In spite of all the breaks she was

111

taking, standing and crouching and standing again, little by little she was making headway.

She heard her sister's voice. Though she wasn't meaning to listen, every word – even the breaths between them – reached her as distinctly as a whisper in her ear. Already more than ten yards ahead, the two older women were in a thicket. She flushed at what she heard and heaved a sigh. It would be too awkward to stand up now. Thankful for the concealment the grass provided, she sat down heavily on the ground, stretched her back, and stroked her big, hard belly. The gesture intensified her shame, and she sweated still more profusely.

' . . . It didn't matter at first. So I didn't say anything in particular, either. Seeing as how she's always been that way . . . different. Not much could surprise me, coming from her.'

She could hear her mother's answer, too:

'Oh, dear me, yes. When *was* that?'

'I was in junior high, so . . . she would have been eight or nine, I'd say.'

'We bought them at the Great Kannon fair. She was so insistent . . . '

'Bursting into tears in front of the stall.'

'That's right. I wasn't too keen on the creepy things, but they were only tiny, and I didn't think they'd last long. How much did we pay for them? . . . Anyway, I bought her a pair, male and female. In a blue cage with a red exercise wheel. I seem to remember them hard at work spinning that wheel. The two of them took turns.'

'What nasty pink tails they had. And she'd happily let them crawl over her body.'

'But she did take good care of them.'

'They don't need much, those things. And in return they have babies, babies, and more babies. A new litter every month or so. I'd always wondered why their name meant "twenty-day mouse". It made me scared to go near her when she had all those baby mice like red beans wriggling in the bottom of the cage. She'd put one on the palm of her hand and snuggle it up to her cheek. But don't get the idea that she loved them. I always thought it was odd – babies by the dozen, yet she never seemed to have more than ten mice. She was burying them in the garden, that's what, as soon as they got bigger. She calmly took

112

the babies that had a fuzz of white hair and dropped them down a
hole.'

'You saw her?'

With an emphatic nod her sister looked back. The young woman
hastily showed a keen interest in her work. What was in her belly had
started to move.

'That's the way she is . . . '

The sister uprooted another bunch of grass with a sweep of the
sickle in her right hand. The young woman laid both hands on her
belly and closed her eyes. The live thing inside felt to the palms of her
hands like a thin dove.

' . . . I'd always thought she must be donating them to the school.'

'I did my best to forget what I'd seen.'

' . . . I ask you, when have I ever had reason to be proud?'

'Oh, but I – '

'Proud of her, I meant . . . '

The young woman drew a deep breath and resumed work. Her
trembling fingertips lost their grip. She remembered the caged mice
busily mating. And herself sprawled watching. A skinny girl with
narrow eyes. She was always fretting, silently chewing the inside of
her cheek. Why had she been so excited about keeping those mice? In
the end she'd buried every last one alive and thrown out the empty
cage.

She tugged with all her strength at the grass that happened to be in
her hand. It broke off at the root. The children came without warning
from behind her and bounded as quickly out of sight again. Her sister
gave a long-drawn-out yell:

'Put on your *hats*!'

I suppose I would turn out like this, after a childhood like that, she
mused, biting her cheek between her back teeth in the old way. She
remembered the man again. She could only remember him smiling.
When they were together face to face, she was always happy. That
was enough, and she'd been thankful, or tried to be. She would find it
strange – exhilaratingly strange – every time she saw the man, who
wasn't supposed to be there, in her room. The man was kind. He held
her tenderly as he inadvertently spoke the name of the woman with
whom he lived. She liked to go to sleep with her cheek pressed to his

113

meagre chest. He bore the weight and let her do what she pleased. She always woke once at first light, convinced the man wouldn't be there. But there he was at her side, as lifelike as could be, breathing deeply in sleep. She wasn't easily persuaded that he was real, and with her right hand would dreamily trace every detail of his body.

Searching for the root she'd left in the ground, the young woman swung the sickle. Its blade struck a stone with a painful scrape. The movements in her belly gave no sign of stopping. Sweat crawled like insects down the insides of her thighs.

Her mother's laugh rang out.

'Neatly in two! Look . . . '

'Well, will you look at that! It's still moving.' Her sister too was excited.

'There must be a nest of them, we've come across such a lot.'

'Think how many we've killed since this morning . . . Kids, we've found another snake. Come here and you can have it!'

Far off the children could be heard shouting with glee. The young woman half rose and craned her neck. Her sister stood in a thicket, in her hands the two halves of a black snake's body which she brandished above her head. They might have been semaphore flags. The children's voices drew nearer. The young woman lowered herself to the ground and wiped the sweat from her face. Her throat was parched. When would they let her go into the house? She couldn't wait. The children's cries of 'Snake, snake!' beat noisily at her ears, then faded leaving a rustle of leaves.

'Always the slowpoke, isn't she? She's away over there.'

When she lifted her face her eyes met those of her mother, who stood staring in her direction. The young woman smiled and hurriedly set to work scything. There's no time to rest, she told herself. Before she knew it the gap between her and the others had widened to over thirty yards. And even her mother and sister weren't halfway across the rank garden yet. By the time they struggled to the far edge it would surely have grown as tall again behind their backs. They wouldn't escape this work all summer long. But perhaps, she felt, because we're women it can't be helped. I'm back on my mother's territory now. Her hard breathing sounded hot and stuffy in her own ears – and even they had sweat trickling inside.

114

Her mother and sister returned to their conversation. The young woman pressed on with the job, almost rubbing her face among the roots. Like her palms, it was smeared and scratched by grass blades. As if in answer to the carrying voices she murmured under her breath: I'm being steeped in the ways of the grass thickets too.

'... The shame I felt – every time I went along to the school they'd want to have a word with me. In the end I stopped going to open days and the PTA. When you were at school, I used to hold my head high.'

'It was no fun for me, either. My teacher and the headmaster were always making cracks. "Doesn't your little sister have a tongue?" or "When's she going to wake up?" or "You must have sucked up all the goodness before you were born." . . . Thank heavens I was only at the same school for a year after she started. On my last day she hung around me with that dopey expression, and since it was the last time I shut her in the turkey's coop in the playground. *That* made her cry. Such a hangdog way of crying she had, too, glancing up at you as she sniffled. I didn't feel the least bit sorry for her.'

'And her skin – there was always something wrong with it. That puffy look it had, all the way to the tips of her fingers, and the sores, and the warts.'

'That's right. She always seemed to have a dirty bandage on. Scraps of sticking plaster dangling under her nose.'

Her sister laughed, and her mother too. Her sister had been top of the class right through school, and was also a strikingly beautiful girl.

She had always wanted to be liked by this sister of hers. She had never doubted that she was inferior in every respect. That went without saying.

A grasshopper jumped out from the leaves of the plant she had uprooted. She caught it swiftly and crushed it in her hand. A small quantity of brown liquid leaked out. Her belly was bloated and her breathing laboured.

'Imagine a girl like that falling for a man, though.'

'But surely that's the whole point: some man only had to use a little flattery and she'd fall for him head over heels. Even now, I'll bet she's quite pleased with herself, if the truth be known.'

'That's going too far.'

Don't you remember, Mother? One New Year's holiday, she decked herself out in my old party dress and stuck a big pink ribbon on her head and was grinning away till I told her what a fright she looked and sent her off smartly to change. So she gave me a dreadful scowl and said, "Well, what did you expect?" Always ready to feel sorry for herself, and my goodness she could be stubborn. After all that, she went straight off and changed out of the dress. Such a stubborn child.'

'She'd never apologise, would she? Or show respect. She's the same way still . . . She was in all her teachers' bad books and never made any friends. Once in a while a child in her class would take pity on her and invite her home, but it never came to anything. She'd keep to herself and stare crossly at the others. Children understand these things best, you know. They never included her in their games, right from the word go. They seemed to be saying it's enough that we're letting you sit there. Remember that time – she was in kindergarten, wasn't she? – she was invited to a party when a child in her class had got over pneumonia. She came back as moody as ever, and didn't have a thing to say. Just when I was thinking, "Oh dear", the mother who'd given the party phoned. Said she didn't remember inviting her. Then she added with a polite laugh that she wouldn't really have minded, except that the girl simply sneered at all their efforts to have her join in their games and raffles. After a while they lost interest and she wandered off by herself. She must have gone through the cupboards and drawers, because when she came back she was triumphantly carrying the mother's underwear and her sanitary napkin belt, which she laid out on the floor for a good look. Perhaps it shouldn't have mattered since she was a girl, the mother said, but she was upset, and after snatching the things back she sent her on her way, rather than scold her. It seems she went quietly, but I just didn't know how to apologise – I couldn't have said why it was such a disgrace, and that made it all the more embarrassing. I could never face that mother again.'

' . . . Now that you mention it, my belt met the same fate. Honestly, what can you say? And what about the time when the neighbours caught her peeping into their bathroom? They had a daughter of twenty or thereabouts . . . '

116

'She certainly could be a pest . . . but I thought she'd grow out of it naturally.'

'Oh no, it's not that simple.'

' . . . She's past hope, you mean. But then *we* have to pick up after her.'

'She's got this attitude that she doesn't count. She thinks she can do what she likes because she'll never amount to anything anyway . . . It's a dirty trick. She does what she pleases, won't take responsibility, then comes slinking back with a pitiful look. Always playing for sympathy.'

'It could simply be that she's stupid, don't you think?'

'Oh, no doubt about that. Look at her appalling grades.'

'She was a lovely bouncing baby. I thought I was bringing her up just like you.'

'It's her nature, that's what . . . '

'Her nature . . . '

'Yes . . . I've thought so for quite some time.'

' . . . How old is she, now?'

'She must be, ah, twenty-four . . . the age I was when I had my first child.'

'That's right . . . '

The mother's sigh reached even her younger daughter's ears. She wiped her brimming tears with the back of a hand stained with earth and grass, but the gesture only brought fresh tears. She wanted to fling her heavy body about in the thickets and cry at the top of her voice. There seemed no other way to relieve her feelings. What was in her belly had grown more active – she could see signs of movement even through her clothes. She placed the sickle on her knees and covered her face with her hands. She was tired. Her body flamed red in the light directly overhead. Where her palm pressed against her lips the flesh was salty. It also smelled of insect.

Memories of childhood pleasures ran through her mind. In summer, sprinkling each other in their bathing suits with the garden hose. Her sister was good at making a rainbow hang in the air. Then there were the canna lilies, scarlet sage, cockscomb, and four-o'clocks that flowered in the garden. Fireworks on summer nights. Walks with her mother. Her mother had taught her to name a few of

117

the constellations: the Scorpion, the Harp, the Swan. Patches of wasteland in the neighbourhood where she'd learned to eat berries. The music box her mother bought her. Inside, she'd locked away a treasured pebble, a flat black stone which took on more lustre with each polishing.

Her sister's clear laughter echoed, followed by shouts from the children which she didn't catch. To ease the unbearable fullness of her abdomen she tried getting down on her hands and knees, then lying flat on her back. She'd never make up the distance now, even if she raced. If she closed her eyes she'd probably fall asleep. The bright red of the dress at her door came suddenly to mind, and she wondered nostalgically what those two were doing. She had no idea how long ago it had all happened. It felt rather like a childhood memory. The weariness that had grated inside her like sand grains dissolved into the smell of the grass. She'd lost all inclination to get back up and swing the sickle. What's the point? she thought. It's past hope – and, realising those were the very words her mother had used, the daughter smiled. The tears spilled over. She blew at an insect flying round the end of her nose. The insect hastily sought the grass thicket from which it had come.

She remembered one more thing from her childhood. She always took baths with her mother. Her mother would wash her back, firmly applying her left hand to the cleft of her buttocks while she scrubbed with her right. The left hand tickled, and the daughter would squirm and roll about laughing. There was always a lizard adhering to the bathroom windowpanes. Why, she wondered desolately, were these childish things returning to her one by one?

At some point after the man had left her room, she had dreamed of a school picnic. Or, in fact, of setting out on the morning of a picnic, for she never did arrive. Her mother wasn't there and she had to get herself ready. She searched the house from top to bottom but could find nothing. She resigned herself to doing without lunch and put her mind to getting dressed. The chest of drawers yielded any number of unfamiliar dresses but not the outfit she was to wear to the picnic. Time was running out – she had to be at the meeting place. She put on just any dress, something of an old-fashioned design, and dashed from the house. As she ran, the dress, which was too big, gradually

118

slipped off. She had nothing on underneath. So there she was, stark naked. That was when she realised she didn't know where to find the meeting place either.

After waking she had spent a long time sifting her memories of school, half convinced something of the kind had actually happened. A silly dream, but one the man mustn't know about under any circumstances. In fact she seldom told him her memories or her dreams. They were fraught with shame.

' . . . It must be getting on for three o'clock,' she heard her sister say. 'I'll go and give the children their tea.'

'All right. I'll soon be finished here . . . '

Startled at the nearness of the voice, she opened her eyes. Her mother was standing beside her. As she scrambled up, the mother said in a low voice, 'Now, now, don't give me more trouble than you have to,' and, pressing her down by the shoulders, squatted with the grass thickets at her back.

She couldn't make out her mother's face in the shadow. The rustling of leaves grew indistinct. Flat on her back on the ground, the daughter smiled up at her. Under her mother's scrutiny she couldn't help feeling her body must be a pathetic sight. She was unable to move. She gazed up at the sky: nothing to see. So it was three o'clock?

The mother touched her daughter's abdomen.

' . . . Seems all right, doesn't it? Well then, I'm going to see about having it out.'

The daughter nodded, and watched the motions of her mother's hands. The time had come sooner than she expected, but – understandably from their point of view – they must want to get this business over with, and it couldn't be helped. Her mother seemed tired too. She began moving her dirt-stained hands with quiet dispatch.

The mother's sweat fell in drops on her abdomen. Having entrusted its handling to her mother, she realised for the first time how acutely she wanted to place a new life in this light-filled outer world. Misshapen though it might be, she wanted it to give a healthy newborn cry. She distrusted her mother's intentions. But she didn't seem able to voice her misgivings. A more suitable place, more care, more time . . . the things she wanted to say stuck in her throat.

Her mother's hands were moving like a small bird's wings. Causing no pain, they made an incision in her abdomen and removed the scallop-like pale pink uterus as easily as they might lift a part from a machine. It was flat and not much more than six inches in diameter. From where the two shells met, there dangled a yellow string. The daughter gazed wretchedly at the object in her mother's hands. Could a thing like that contain a new life? It was impossible to have confidence. If only her mother would say something.

Her mother was silent. Taking her sickle in her right hand she casually cut the string. Judging by its terrible thinness it had been about to break at any moment. That must be what was called the umbilical cord. The daughter's heart sank again at the sight of that tenuous cord, so slender it must surely be hopeless. The two valves were gaping open half an inch. She would find out if she peered inside but she hadn't the courage. Something seemed to be squirming in there, and this was her only comfort. Whatever the daughter's fears, her mother lost no time in prying off the womb-shell's lid with both hands. Though quite stiff, the valves parted at once. Then she drew out a square of red. Beneath it, stuck fast, should be the source of the newborn's cry. So the daughter believed, though she was seeing it for the first time in her life. Tenderly, she held her breath. But her mother took one look, clicked her tongue, and pushed what she alone had seen back into the uterus.

The daughter looked up at her uterus with tears in her eyes. So it hadn't been the right thing to do, after all. They should have known it was too early. But rather than reproaching her mother, she was overwhelmed with tenderness for her tiny womb.

The uterus in her mother's hands shriveled rapidly in the light, little holes pitting its surface like pumice. She wanted to seize it back, but it was past saving now, and she didn't even reach out her hand. When she closed her eyes she could feel the teardrops moving of their own accord over her skin.

Her murmured words could have been the sound of an insect's wings: Yes, past hope.

The voices of her sister's children echoed faintly.

By the time she sat up, her mother was nowhere to be seen. Picking up the sickle lying on the ground, she began to dig at the roots of the

120

grasses. She might as well, as long as she was here. For the present she could think of nothing else to do. She wanted to make amends. She became absorbed in the work.

The daughter was alone in the thickets. She considered the volume of grass: it was her love for her family, for the baby, for the man. It was her love for herself. The ground in which the grasses were rooted was hard as a rock.

AN · EMBRACE

His name meant nothing to me, of course. Perhaps the tension at my end could be felt over the phone, for the unfamiliar voice hurried to add an explanation of sorts. 'Megumi Hirota's . . . '

I caught on then. 'Ah, that Hirota . . . '

It was not Megumi Hirota who came to mind, however; only her death. When Sumiko had rung to tell me that Megumi Hirota had died, I had vaguely recognised the name but couldn't put a face to it at all, and, failing to register the slightest shock, had found myself maintaining a deliberate coolness towards Sumiko throughout the call which she'd made especially to give me this hot news. At another time I might have managed to sound surprised despite a total lack of interest, but I was in no mood even for such politenesses. Sumiko's manner of speaking grated, too, by implying how very well she remembered the dead woman. All the same, I wasn't rude enough to point out that in all likelihood she'd never given her a thought until this happened.

I had spent the three senior years at the same girls' school as both Sumiko and Megumi. But Sumiko and I, straggling into a class that had come up together through elementary school and junior high, had left without ever fitting in with the other girls. Megumi was one of them, and as I didn't see her in the clubs or committees I joined, I don't suppose we had much occasion to speak. As far as I knew, Sumiko had been no better acquainted.

After hearing of Megumi's death I had remained so indifferent that I can only put it down to stubbornness. I might have forgotten her face, but all I would have had to do was find the twenty-year-old class

122

photograph that I had saved, and it would have been easy enough to identify her. Yet it hadn't even occurred to me. Why insist on remembering and undo the favour someone had done me by dying when I'd already forgotten her, so that I needn't feel a thing? I'm not that big a fool, I had told myself, restraining the urge to remember what she was like.

There I was, then, struggling to work out how long ago I'd heard the news from Sumiko, when Megumi's husband did the arithmetic for me.

'It was last spring. It's been eight months.'

'Has it?'

'I've made a start on trying to sort her things. She left them in a mess, so it's quite a job.'

'Yes, it must be . . .'

All I could do was make feeble comments in return. Not having attended the funeral, nor in fact given a thought to the family, I was finding it difficult now to offer my sympathy to the bereaved husband. One thing was clear, though: my studied indifference to Megumi's death had been abruptly shattered by this sudden phone call from her husband. With Hirota on the line in person one couldn't avoid considering his special position, and I was shaken and flustered by the difficulty of finding a tactful response. Gripping the receiver nervously, I hadn't time to wonder what business he had with me.

'Things keep turning up. There seems no end to them. Old yearbooks and so on. I don't like to throw them out . . .'

'I see . . .'

'And so I was wondering if we could meet, just briefly. Would you mind?' There was no tension in his voice; perhaps its being rather high-pitched for a man's made him sound so nonchalant.

'Meet? You mean, you and I?' I was growing more flustered.

'Yes. In an hour from now, say? It will take me about that long to get over there.'

'An hour? . . . You mean . . . does it have to be right away?'

'No?'

'Well, I wouldn't say that, but . . .'

'Then you don't mind? You decide the place. Where do you want me to be? If you know a coffee shop, for example . . .'

'I'm afraid I don't really . . . '

'Then shall I come to your neighbourhood?'

'Oh no, you needn't – '

'I don't mind at all. Am I right in thinking from your address that the nearest station would be Ikebukuro?'

Not stopping to think I answered, 'No, it's three beyond Ikebukuro.' And though I still didn't know what was going on, I gave him the name of a coffee shop near the station.

The moment I put down the receiver my heart began to pound. I was at home on a Saturday afternoon, but what about Hirota, was he proposing to make a special trip from home? Or had he phoned from an office? My twelve-year-old was at a friend's place and wouldn't be back till around seven. As just the two of us lived together, nothing prevented my going to meet Hirota. I had been sleepily stretched out under the quilt covering the foot warmer when he had phoned. It was only in the last year or two, now my daughter was older, that I'd had that kind of time to myself.

I thought of not going – yet could find no cause for the wariness I felt. My alarm was probably selfish whim. Hirota must have something he wanted to tell me, or get me to tell someone else, in connection with Megumi. Though I couldn't imagine what.

I'd dithered till the hour was nearly up. I changed just my skirt, put on make-up, and went to the coffee shop. It was less than ten minutes' walk from my apartment. As I hurried there I went back over what I'd heard from Sumiko: that Megumi had died not of illness but of sleeping pills, for reasons unknown; that she left two children, both fairly young; that Megumi's husband had quit a large corporation several years earlier to become a salesman for a line of English teaching materials; that the change in circumstances may have had some bearing on Megumi's death . . .

Maybe Hirota wanted to see me as part of his job. I was a little more comfortable once I'd hit on this. He might have noted that his wife's contemporaries had children in their early teens and tried us one by one, pushing those expensive sets of texts and tapes. People who attended the funeral might have been moved to buy out of sympathy. Yes, that could be it; in which case poor Hirota would be making a wasted trip – surely not the first. The least I could do was look friendly. I seized on this explanation to set my mind at ease.

124

I'd been to the coffee shop once or twice for a sandwich, with my daughter. As it faced onto the main road and was longer than it was deep, the interior was light. I wasn't confident of picking out Hirota, never having met him, but at my approach the only fortyish man sitting alone got up with a smile. Yes, his name was Hirota.

'I'm sorry to have called you so . . . ' he began.

I put in, 'Oh, no, that's all right,' and we did without further introductions. Sitting down, I glanced quickly around the other tables: luckily, there was no one I recognised from the neighbourhood.

He had a long, narrow face with high cheekbones. His expression gave no more sign of nerves than his relaxed tone had done on the telephone, his pleasant smile seeming to bear out my impression that this was 'business'. He had no obvious grey hairs, nor was he particularly thin; his dress was casual, a dark blue zip-up jacket. In short, no trace of Hirota's special situation could be detected in his appearance. I was momentarily disappointed, and then realised that with the experience he'd had in the past months both my curiosity and my disappointment would be completely transparent to Hirota, and at once I lost what little composure I had mustered on the way.

Feeling cornered, I spoke first. 'Er . . . there was something you wanted to see me about?'

Hirota's genial reply, 'Nothing special', left me no more to say.

'Oh . . . ' I wondered whether this pussyfooting might be a sales technique; but – in my mid-thirties, with a child in junior high – I still wasn't adult enough to go on chatting noncommittally until I saw what he was after.

Taking no notice of my discomfort, Hirota said, 'It's the first time I've gotten off at this station. After all the years I've been in Tokyo, there are still plenty of stations on the Yamanote Line where I've never gotten off. Have you lived here long? Since you were a child?'

' . . . Yes, I've always lived here.'

'You're living in the house where you grew up?'

'No . . . ah, not in the same house.'

'But close to home.'

'That's right . . . It's nearby. But I did move further away at one time.'

'Where was that?'

I named a station on a suburban line where I'd lived while married, before my daughter started school. I wondered how much longer Hirota intended to go on putting these questions and told myself there was really no need to go on answering like a simpleton, but at the same time I was grateful for a line of questioning that was so specific. And Hirota's evident interest in the answers was certainly flattering. People didn't usually ask about these things and I never had any reason to bring them up myself. While I was replying, I had forgotten to give any further thought to Hirota.

He nodded on hearing the station's name: he'd lived in that area himself. 'I was still single at the time,' he went on. 'Would you have been there then?'

'No, I'd been married . . . three or four years. That makes it . . . about ten years ago.'

'Then I was there briefly ahead of you. Were you there long?'

'About four years. Before coming back here.'

Hirota's smile broadened. 'So you preferred to have your family handy, after all?'

'Well, yes,' I conceded at last; I'd had to overcome my embarrassment to answer. Privately, I was offering the excuse that I hadn't actually gone home to Mother, despite the general insistence that it was the normal thing to do, and Mother's own pleading.

'I suppose one would. Is your husband a Tokyo man?'

' . . . No, but we'd separated, you see, by the time I came back here . . .'

I remembered the membership lists for our class reunions: the few unchanged surnames drew attention to themselves. Hirota, however, wasn't likely to have looked very closely, and in fact I couldn't be sure that Megumi herself had kept up with my movements.

'Ah . . . I see. Then you have a job?' Matter-of-factly – to my relief – he asked another practical question.

'Yes . . . I was already working, and so I just kept on.'

'What kind of work do you do? Are you a schoolteacher?'

I shook my head with a slight smile. Through the plate glass beside me I could see a willow at the street's edge. The leaves, slow to yellow and to fall, shone in the full light of the late afternoon sun with a color that evoked nostalgia. Hirota, too, had turned his gaze to the window as he drank water from his glass.

'Do I look like one?'

He nodded. 'And sound like one.'

'Oh no. This is just . . . I work in an office. The sort of office that will give someone like me a job.'

'What do you mean, someone like you?' His tone was teasing. I noticed then that he had a mole beneath his eye. Now that I looked properly, his face had a surprising number of moles.

'Sloppy, uncooperative, always making mistakes . . . '

'Is that a fact?' Hirota broke into a grin.

'Yes, it is. I even drive myself up the wall.'

'It must be difficult for you, though?'

'What do you mean, difficult?' I said sharply, hiding embarrassment.

'I mean, you've raised your daughter single-handed, haven't you?'

'But . . . that's something I brought on myself.' I could tell I was blushing. I wasn't accustomed to such simple appreciation of the work that went into my day-to-day life.

Still smiling, Hirota came out suddenly with the question, 'Why did you get married?'

'Why? . . . I was determined to get away from home. As long as I stayed there I would always be treated like a child. It was to get away.'

'Ah. I suppose it's like that for a girl. Were you always arguing?'

'Yes . . . Though it was worse than arguing, actually . . . There was only my mother and me, you see, so we couldn't help getting claustrophobic . . . '

Then all at once it hit me and I stared at Hirota. He bent his head in assent. Unnerved, I lowered my eyes. It was strange: why hadn't I noticed sooner? The discovery brought back a sensation I had often known at school, the sense that however tough I tried to act the strength drained through the soles of my feet while my body's surface seemed to desiccate and go rigid. Though I never let myself take that sensation too seriously, of course, for if I did I'd be finished. Instead I would even tell my classmates the truth about my father's death, recklessly, defiantly, as if it weren't important. Yet there were

127

episodes – a teacher at junior high, for example, reducing me to stammering confusion when she happened to ask the cause of my father's death in front of the whole class – which in my bitterness I still couldn't seem to forget.

I had also remembered something about Sumiko. Her mother, too, had taken an overdose. Sumiko was sixteen at the time. The rumour had naturally spread overnight, and all kinds of surmises were whispered back and forth at school. But my clearest memory was not of the whispered talk, nor Sumiko's own account of what had happened, but rather a half-glimpsed scene that occurred some time after her mother's funeral. Sumiko must have been on cleaning duty, because she was alone after school at the washbasins rinsing the cloth she'd used. The others had long since left theirs to dry, and I remember seeing her back view and thinking how slow she always was. I don't remember, though, whether I was going up to Sumiko to speak to her or merely passing by.

The Englishwoman coming down the corridor in the other direction had also noticed Sumiko there alone. This elderly teacher was popular with her pupils, and like everyone else I felt an enthusiasm for her English classes that I lacked in other subjects. The teacher came up to Sumiko from behind and, without a word, put her arms around her shoulders and hugged her to her breast. Sumiko looked startled, but when she saw who it was she lowered her face shyly and let herself be held.

The embrace lasted just four or five seconds. But the jealousy it stirred in me persisted. If the Englishwoman's sympathy for Sumiko had been expressed in words I could have let it pass, but it had taken the form of an embrace, and this made it much harder to be dispassionate. Never mind what other people thought about Sumiko's bereavement: why should *I* recognise that she had had an experience meriting such a special gesture? After losing her mother, at least Sumiko was still assured, wasn't she, that her livelihood would go on as before? Everybody's parents die once, so in a sense it was nothing extraordinary. And as Sumiko was already in senior high school, her parents had more or less played their part, hadn't they? In any case Sumiko was so nearly an adult that people shouldn't start babying her because of this . . .

Yet part of me wanted to protest to the English teacher: if she hugged Sumiko, why not me? It was years since my father had died, but I was still a child in the same circumstances as Sumiko, and just as entitled to a hug. I hung back in timid anticipation: wouldn't she at least think to look my way, saying, 'Oh, dear, did it happen to you, too?'

The death of Sumiko's mother seems to have meant very little to me in the end. It aroused not my sympathy but my jealousy. Throughout our later acquaintance, I don't remember our ever comforting each other or sharing our emotions. I still considered her lucky, attracting sympathy in that form.

When she phoned me with the news about Megumi, for that matter, there was nothing in Sumiko's voice to suggest that it had brought back her mother's death.

In the silence which I had allowed to fall, Hirota said in an abstracted way, 'She was talking about you, quite a while ago. It's funny, one remembers these things more than you'd expect . . . '

Then she hadn't forgotten the stories about me. I wondered what Megumi had told him, but couldn't bring myself to ask. If Hirota had been brooding over some remark of hers, to ask might open a real can of worms. I decided to think only of Hirota's two children. There was nothing else I could do, in any case.

'There was another girl in our class, you know, who lost one of her parents in the same way. When my father died I wasn't old enough to understand what happened, but in her case it must have been . . . '

'Yes, I know what you mean. My children are young, too – one's only four. They're both girls.'

Following Hirota's eyes, I glanced out the window again. The willow tree was no longer shining. The sky was still bright but the ground had turned the colour of twilight.

'I don't think you need to worry about the children. Wouldn't it be better, for their sakes, not to pity them or make a special fuss?' I was urgently searching the dim reaches of my childhood self: if I must say something to Hirota, then at least it mustn't be far from what I felt. 'As a child I accepted the fact calmly. You see, there was no other way to think of it but as a fact . . . It was only later, when I was old enough to understand other people's reactions, that I couldn't take it

129

so calmly. People embellished the story in ways that didn't agree with the facts, and I became very upset . . . I thought I could count on my mother since she knew the facts, but it wasn't a pleasant feeling to learn that she was actually sorry for me. Because personally I couldn't have cared less . . . or rather, I don't suppose I could afford to feel sorry for myself . . . '

'Does that mean you weren't calm, really?' said Hirota with a smile.

'No, that's not what I meant . . . I was only interested in the here and now, not in what had happened . . . Children are like that. I see it in my own daughter . . . You needn't worry about them, truly.'

'Well, I have to admit I'm not all that worried. I've got too much else on my mind. If someone were to offer to take my children right now, I might be delighted to hand them over. That's how unworried I am . . . And so, what made you strike out on your own?'

Words failed me again. The things this man had the nerve to ask! But I couldn't pretend not to have heard.

' . . . I'm too quick to fall in love. I tend to be that way . . . I rushed into marriage without even trying to see what sort of person he was, with only my feelings to go by . . . Having lost my father, I suspect that somehow I may not be able to think realistically about men . . . You needn't worry about your daughters, though. Their father's very much alive.'

At that point six or seven women in their fifties entered in a noisy group. On their way home from some sort of dressy occasion, they were in such high spirits that their normal reserve towards other customers was forgotten.

'I wonder if I *am* very much alive?' Hirota smiled wryly.

'You look healthy – very.'

'I suppose so.' He nodded, and glanced at the women who had changed the coffee shop's atmosphere. 'We've been here nearly an hour. You may go now.'

His abruptness startled me, but I saw no need for hesitation, either. Murmuring 'Well, then', I rose halfway out of my seat and took the purse from my bag.

'I'll pay. You can go.'

For the first time he spoke brusquely. As I hovered in indecision,

130

Hirota took the check from the table in his right hand, stood up, and whispered, 'Did you think me strange? Did my behaviour offend you?'

'No,' I answered quickly. 'I didn't think anything of your behaviour. I don't know the first thing about you.'

'Ah. Yes, I suppose that's right.' He regained his smile as if convinced by this, and sat down. He seemed to have come empty-handed, for there was nothing of his in sight.

'Well, then . . . er . . . good luck.' Awkwardly, I bowed and walked on out of the coffee shop.

I didn't expect to encounter Hirota again. Our meeting had started me remembering a string of small details which, to my vexation, I couldn't get out of my mind. But my preoccupation was not with Hirota. The way we met had been odd, admittedly, yet when I considered that except for Megumi's death we'd have had no cause to meet, I asked myself how else it could have come about. No, Hirota had set me thinking about Sumiko.

Sumiko and I still kept up well enough to stay current with each other's news. In the twenty years since high school we'd sometimes seen more of each other, sometimes less, but – while I wouldn't say we hit it off especially well – we never lost contact altogether. Sumiko might call after a long interval and invite me out the next time she came into the city, or, with my daughter away for several days on a school outing, I might call and suggest a movie. Since Sumiko's two children were older than my daughter, I would sometimes confide my anxieties about schoolwork or ask her about an infection that didn't seem to warrant a trip to the doctor. When our children were smaller we used to visit each other's homes, and she would pass on their outgrown clothes. Sumiko didn't change towards me once I was on my own. Whenever we met there was no lack of subjects that we two women could talk over at our ease; then, having caught up, we might not see each other for six months or a year.

There had been times, though, when my end of the conversation dragged. Sumiko had a husband in a solid profession and considered home and family her occupation. By comparison, with my constant worries about time and money, I would feel so inadequate that I'd even contemplate not seeing her again. What impression I made on Sumiko I couldn't say, but whenever I saw her face I would be reminded that for twenty years I'd thought how very different she was from me.

Why, then, had we kept on and on probing into what was happening in our lives? Because what bound us together was the unnatural death of a parent. Only after meeting Hirota did I realise this; strange as it may seem, I had actually forgotten what we had in common. It had somehow been reduced to a trivial occurrence of a past era, entirely beneath our notice. To the two of us whose lives had gone on, our children's cold sores and the mildew on the bathroom tiles were more pressing shared concerns.

Or so I told myself. There could be no point in discussing what could yield no sense of reality now even if we were to try; we had other things to discuss. Of course, the same could be said of talking to my mother, but I couldn't compare my one surviving parent and Sumiko. My association with Sumiko was tinged with guilt; I would have liked to avert my eyes, if I could, from our shamefaced inability to let our interest in each other's lives drop.

I was afraid that since I'd met Hirota the belated awareness of this bond might make it awkward to see Sumiko again. There was no reason why it should, however: doubtless the next time I heard Sumiko's voice I would very naturally shut away the long-ago deaths of her mother and my father, exactly as I had always done, and launch instead into a lament about my daughter's poor arithmetic marks or complaints about my problems on the job.

When Hirota phoned again, about a month had passed. It was on the night before Christmas Eve, at an hour when I had to get to bed. I had taken a bath and was in pyjamas, drying my hair. My daughter, allowed up past ten o'clock now that she was in junior high, was already asleep.

Late-night phone calls were so rare that I automatically expected the worst, so that when I heard that same casual voice say, 'It's Hirota. Thanks for the other day,' I relaxed in sheer relief.

Hirota asked, 'How would you like to meet me for a drink? I was in a bar in another part of town, but I remembered you, and to tell the truth I'm already in your neighbourhood. Do you mind?'

132

Since he'd effectively headed me off it was difficult to say I minded. I did try to wriggle out of it with 'I was about to go to bed' or 'I haven't been drinking much lately', but Hirota wasn't impressed.

'Just for half an hour. I won't want to drink much more, in any case.' And so I found myself obliged to go out. Getting dressed was a lot of bother, and in view of the hour it seemed to me I'd been altogether too hasty in agreeing to his invitation. However, I also wondered whether Hirota mightn't have asked to see me again because he couldn't leave unanswered something I'd said last time; if so, I felt I couldn't escape his displeasure, or anger, or resentment (though a thrill of curiosity may also have been at work). Purely because I'd assumed I would never meet Hirota again, I'd got by without giving him another thought: now I was nervous about the attitude I'd taken and what I had said. Could it have been presumptuous? Had I come out with some thoughtless remark? As I myself had no intention of seeing Hirota again, it had suited me to consider the matter closed for him as well.

Hirota was waiting in front of my building. We began walking side by side towards the station.

'You really have just got out of the bath, haven't you?' Hirota laughed.

I glared at him and retorted, 'I'll catch cold with this wet hair.'

'It's not that cold today, is it? During the daytime it was nice and warm.' Hirota was wearing a raincoat over a suit and carrying an old Boston bag. He was just a little taller than me.

'You're warm because you've been drinking, Mr Hirota.'

'Is that it? . . . Then you'll be all right when you've had a few yourself. I'm sure you *can* drink, can't you?'

'No, I can't take much.'

Chatting about this and that, we went into a bar-and-grill in an alley by the station. They closed at twelve, we were informed, but as that was an hour off we took seats anyway, side by side at the counter. There were only a couple of other customers. The cooks appeared more interested in closing up than making us welcome, and as they even begrudged us the heating we were not encouraged to take off our coats and make ourselves comfortable. We each ordered skewers of chicken and hot saké.

Hirota began to talk about his job. Megumi had taught the piano at home. The income she brought in had been substantial, and it seemed Hirota had unconsciously come to rely on his wife's earnings, and as a result he had become self-indulgent. He had decided to leave his previous company, where they worked him very hard, to take a more flexible job as a salesman while he studied translation on the side. This was an ambition of his younger days. He had learned the ropes in a college society. Of course he hoped eventually to make his living at it, but he had to admit he'd been too soft on himself in thinking they could fall back on his wife's earnings if he should fail. Now, with those earnings cut off, he was looking for a new job in order to support the two children by himself.

'I've found one opening, but at my age, you know, even if they take me the conditions won't be good. At the moment we're at my parents' house, which is a big help, but . . . '

'So that's how a family man like you can hang out in bars till all hours of the night? Not like me.' I spoke lightly, for I had guessed as much.

'Hang out? You could call it that. There's nothing for me to do at home . . . ' Hirota made a joke of it while staring me in the face.

I hastened to explain. 'You see, when my daughter was younger it was hard being tied down to her and to my job, never having any breathing space to myself. For me that was the hardest part, and so I thought . . . '

'I know what you mean . . . But you're able to afford a decent apartment on your own. That's quite something.'

'Decent? It's only two rooms.'

'Is that right?'

'And besides . . . you'll probably have the chance to remarry, but that's more than I can expect. My prospects are all mapped out: I'll simply go on like this till I turn forty, then fifty . . . '

Hirota looked serious. 'I don't want to get married again . . . I'll bet you don't either, do you, really?'

After a moment's thought I shook my head. 'I used to dream, now and then, but that was two or three years ago . . . '

'I don't want to get married, but I could do with a woman in my life.'

134

'Oh, I could do with someone too!' I laughed, and Hirota joined in.

'Is there anyone?' he asked.

'I'm afraid not . . . It's not easy to find someone who'll take a liking to my child, someone who'll take a liking to me, and someone who'll take a liking to us both, all in one. And you?' I was speaking far too freely – beginning to feel the saké's effects.

'No, me neither. Though there was someone I fooled around with a while back.'

'You must be lonely, then . . . Not for long, I'm sure. But I expect it won't be quite the same for the children.'

'Oh, they hardly appear to have noticed. Just as you said,' Hirota murmured without much interest.

'Yes . . . though I do feel there is some strange effect on the children, after all . . . Since last time, I've started remembering . . . '

'What?' As if more concerned about closing time than his children, Hirota was gazing around the now empty restaurant.

' . . . The water model. I can't seem to get it out of my mind . . . A model that shows you the life cycle of water. It'd be four years ago, now – my daughter and I discovered it in the roof garden of a department store. It was huge, but most people missed it. I suppose because it was behind plastic panels. There was a snow-capped mountain, and the melting snow turned into a river as it flowed down the slopes where there were orchards, past farms where people were working in the fields, past a school . . . And a model railway ran through a tunnel right under the mountain . . . Then the river came to rice fields at the foot of the mountain, and I think there might have been cattle grazing too. Then a suburban housing development, and then the city. Rows of tall buildings, and expressways, and on the expressways were miniature cars. Then the water flowed through an industrial belt, and finally it made its way to the coast . . . There was a good area of sea, and the harbour had ferries and fishing boats floating in it . . . Live goldfish swimming in it, too. Yes, now I remember . . . Because of course the river was real water. Trickling from the mountain-top to the sea. One of those models . . . '

'I think we'd better be going,' Hirota interrupted, 'they're looking our way.' I glanced around: he was right. I got up and went outside. Hirota took care of the bill. As soon as he came out of the bar I started right in where I'd left off, talking fast.

'It gave me an eerie feeling, you know, when I saw it. Very eerie – '

'I'll walk you to your apartment,' said Hirota. I nodded and continued:

'My daughter took such a fancy to it, she began making models herself. I did think it was on a grand scale, but that would have been all – if she hadn't insisted we go back later for another look. By then it was gone, only the base was left . . . It was such a relief not to have to look at that scary thing again. I wonder whether everyone gets that feeling – a kind of faintness, as if something inside you were being sucked out? I'm not sure, but lately – in fact since I met you, Mr Hirota – I've remembered other things too . . . Model trains in the toy department used to give me that same eerie feeling, and once at elementary school I saw an exhibit the mothers had brought in, a town made out of sugar. It had masses of fine detail. I was afraid yet couldn't seem to leave. That model was the same: it made me feel like crying, like dissolving away. Nostalgic, and sad, and enchanted . . . a dreamy sort of feeling.'

I broke off and looked at Hirota's face. He said in a low, embarrassed voice, 'Mind if we walk like this?' and put his arm around my shoulders. As we were some distance apart this made it a little difficult to walk. There was no one else on the street.

'You know how looking over the edge of a rooftop makes your head spin? It's a bit similar. I liked going up on the roof at school, and I'd look down and think "If I fell, I'd die, wouldn't I?" Death seemed very close, and it made me shiver. It's the same looking at those models. It doesn't seem to be the model I'm afraid of, but myself. Because I become one of the dead . . . One sees with the eyes of the dead, you know, when one looks down at a model. There's a nostalgia there, too, and an enchantment . . . '

As Hirota had come to a halt, I did likewise. Too soon, we'd arrived in front of the building where I lived. Hirota's arm left my shoulders.

'I'm sorry to have brought up a touchy subject like this. I'm not sure what I'm trying to say . . . You know, when I heard about Megumi I wasn't even surprised. Nor when others have died. I'm quite unmoved. I can't take people's dying seriously enough. Since my father chose to approach death himself, I seem to have made up my mind that death was an intimate of mine. "Death" and "parent" may have taken on the same meaning for me, even though my father was only my father as long as he was alive . . . It's a silly illusion I've always had . . . '

I glanced behind me at the glass doors of the building. We shouldn't stand outside talking too long. I turned back to Hirota and let out a sigh. 'It's odd, though, isn't it, talking to you like this when I hardly remember Megumi . . . ?'

'I don't mind a bit,' Hirota answered with a smile. I wished I could have invited him in.

' . . . It doesn't matter, though . . . Well, then – ' At the same instant, my body was caught in a strong force. I stared wide-eyed. Hirota was holding me tight. He was pressing his cheek against mine. Before my eyes was his ear lobe, reddened slightly. His cheek and body were soft and warm. I relaxed and wrapped my arms around him. The sound of our hearts reverberated.

'Not here . . . ' I whispered to his ear lobe. Hirota nodded silently without taking his cheek from mine. 'If the neighbours see us . . . '

I heard his muffled voice. 'Never mind. Just a little longer.'

Closing my eyes, I stroked his back. His raincoat, cold in the night air, turned warm at once.

I heard him sigh. He moved his cheek away and touched mine with his lips. I did the same. My lips brought the sensation of his skin more pleasantly than my cheek had done. Our faces gradually met and we put our lips together. We made sure how our tongues felt, too. Inside his mouth was hot. I wanted us to undress there and then and assure ourselves of the other parts of our bodies.

I opened my eyes and stared at Hirota's face close in front of mine. He noticed and moved his face away. He asked, 'Are you going?' I nodded. With a sigh, he rubbed his cheek against mine once more.

'That feels very good,' I murmured, trying to catch my breath. My voice didn't come out too well.

'Does it?' he said in the same voice.

'Yes, truly . . . but, listen, I'm going now . . . ' I managed to say it, and separated myself from Hirota's arms.

'You're going home?' He looked confused. I nodded, in confusion myself. My legs were shaking.

137

'There's someone else I'm close to – a woman, but . . . we have the same thing in common as you and I . . . That's why . . . '

Hirota nodded though he still looked dazed.

'Well, then, good luck.' With a quick bow of my head, I dashed into the lobby. I pressed the elevator button, and in the moment's pause before the doors opened I glanced behind me. Hirota was still standing in a daze. I could not go back to him. I bowed my head again, stepped into the elevator and pressed the button to close the doors. I was trying to explain, to apologise to him: two of us are bad enough, but if three people huddled together like that I'd be trapped by the eyes for certain. I'm not yet able to forget the eyes of the dead gazing down on us as one would look at a model, and I don't know when I will; for now, all I can do is protect those who are alive by pretending not to have noticed. That is why we must avoid calling to one another, so as to attract as little attention as possible. I must not long for those eyes. I must not even acknowledge their existence. Because in fact there is only a word, 'death'; nothing more. All we ought to know is that those people were once alive, which ought not to give us anything in common . . .

That was nearly a year ago, and there have been no more phone calls from Hirota. I would like to know how he is, but there is no way I can find out. I just go on wondering how he is getting on.

I do keep in touch with Sumiko, as usual. She phoned only last week, and we grumbled over the way our children, though past the age for Christmas presents, go to work on us for expensive things as if taking them for granted. Last year's order was for oil paints, this year's a fully automatic camera. All it amounts to is the birthday of some complete stranger called Christ; yet it doesn't feel at all bad to become a generous giver on that day.

ABOUT THE AUTHOR

Yūko Tsushima built her reputation as a major writer through her short fiction. She published her first story in 1969 while still in college, and twelve collections have appeared in Japan to date. Her story "The Silent Traders," which is included in this book, was awarded the 1983 Yasunari Kawabata Prize. In addition she has written six novels, including *Chōji* (1978), which won the Women's Literature Prize in Japan that year, and in 1983 was published in the United States to excellent reviews under the title *Child of Fortune*. Her most recent novel, *Yoru no hikari ni owarete* (*Driven by the Light of the Night*, 1986), won the Yomiuri Literature Prize.

Yūko Tsushima was born in 1947, the daughter of the celebrated Japanese novelist Osamu Dazai, who committed suicide in 1948. She lives in Tokyo with her daughter.

PANTHEON MODERN WRITERS ORIGINALS

THE VICE-CONSUL
by Marguerite Duras, translated from the French by Eileen Ellenbogen

The first American edition ever of the novel Marguerite Duras considers her best — a tale of passion and desperation set in India and Southeast Asia.

"A masterful novel." — *The Chicago Tribune*
0-394-55898-7 cloth, $10.95   0-394-75026-8 paper, $6.95

MAPS
by Nuruddin Farah

The unforgettable story of one man's coming of age in the turmoil of modern Africa.

"A true and rich work of art . . . [by] one of the finest contemporary African writers."
—Salman Rushdie
0-394-56325-5 cloth, $11.95   0-394-75548-0 paper, $7.95

DREAMING JUNGLES
by Michel Rio, translated from the French by William Carlson

A hypnotic novel about an elegant French scientist and his shattering confrontation in turn-of-the-century Africa with the jungle, passion, and at last, himself.

"A subtle philosophical excursion embodied in a story of travel and adventure. . . . It succeeds extremely well."   — *The New York Times Book Review*
0-394-55661-5 cloth, $10.95   0-394-75035-7 paper, $6.95

BURNING PATIENCE
by Antonio Skármeta, translated from the Spanish by Katherine Silver

A charming story about the friendship that develops between Pablo Neruda, Latin America's greatest poet, and the postman who stops to receive his advice about love.

"The mix of the fictional and the real is masterful, and . . . gives the book its special appeal and brilliance."   — *Christian Science Monitor*
0-394-55576-7 cloth, $10.95   0-394-75033-0 paper, $6.95

YOU CAN'T GET LOST IN CAPE TOWN
by Zoë Wicomb

Nine stories powerfully evoke a young black woman's upbringing in South Africa.

"A superb first collection." — *The New York Times Book Review*
0-394-56030-2 cloth, $10.95   0-394-75309-7 paper, $6.95

THE SHOOTING GALLERY
by Yūko Tsushima, compiled and translated from the Japanese by Geraldine Harcourt

Eight stories about modern Japanese women by one of Japan's finest contemporary writers.

"Tsushima is a subtle, surprising, elegant writer who courageously tells unexpected truths."   —Margaret Drabble
0-394-75743-2 paper, $7.95

THE WINNERS
by Julio Cortázar, translated from the Spanish by Elaine Kerrigan

Julio Cortázar's superb first novel about a South American luxury cruise.

"Irresistibly readable . . . introduces a dazzling writer."
—*The New York Times Book Review*
0-394-72301-5 paper, $8.95

THE LEOPARD
by Giuseppe di Lampedusa, translated from the Italian by Archibald Colquhoun

The world-renowned novel of a Sicilian prince in the turbulent Italy of the 1860s.

"The genius of its author and the thrill it gives the reader are probably for all time."
—*The New York Times Book Review*
0-394-74949-9 paper, $7.95

YOUNG TÖRLESS
by Robert Musil, translated from the German
by Eithne Williams and Ernst Kaiser

A classic novel by the author of *The Man Without Qualities,* about students at an Austrian military academy and their brutality to one another.

"An illumination of the dark places of the heart."—*The Washington Post*
0-394-71015-0 paper, $6.95

ADIEUX: A FAREWELL TO SARTRE
by Simone de Beauvoir, translated from the French by Patrick O'Brian

Simone de Beauvoir's moving farewell to Jean-Paul Sartre: "an intimate, personal, and honest portrait of a relationship unlike any other in literary history." —Deirdre Bair
0-394-72898-X paper, $8.95

THE BLOOD OF OTHERS
by Simone de Beauvoir,
translated from the French by Roger Senhouse and Yvonne Moyse

A brilliant existentialist novel about the French resistance, "with a remarkably sustained note of suspense and mounting excitement."—*Saturday Review*
0-394-72411-9 paper, $7.95

A VERY EASY DEATH
by Simone de Beauvoir, translated from the French by Patrick O'Brian

The profoundly moving, day-by-day account of the death of the author's mother.

"A beautiful book, sincere and sensitive."—Pierre-Henri Simon
0-394-72899-8 paper, $4.95

WHEN THINGS OF THE SPIRIT COME FIRST:
FIVE EARLY TALES
by Simone de Beauvoir, translated from the French by Patrick O'Brian

The first paperback edition of the marvelous early fiction of Simone de Beauvoir.

"An event for celebration."—*The New York Times Book Review*
0-394-72235-3 paper, $6.95

THE WOMAN DESTROYED
by Simone de Beauvoir, translated from the French by Patrick O'Brian

Three powerful stories of women in crisis by the legendary novelist and feminist.

"Immensely intelligent stories about the decay of passion."
—*The* [London] *Sunday Times*
0-394-71103-3 paper, $7.95

THE ASSAULT
by Harry Mulisch, translated from the Dutch by Claire Nicolas White

The story of a Nazi atrocity in Occupied Holland and its impact on the life of one survivor.

"Brilliant . . . stunningly rendered."—John Updike
0-394-74420-9 paper, $6.95

THE WALL JUMPER
by Peter Schneider, translated from the German by Leigh Hafrey

A powerful, witty novel of life in modern Berlin.

"Marvelous . . . creates, in very few words, the unreal reality of Berlin."
—Salman Rushdie, *The New York Times Book Review*
0-394-72882-3 paper, $6.95

FRIDAY
by Michel Tournier, translated from the French by Norman Denny

A sly retelling of the story of Robinson Crusoe.

"A fascinating, unusual novel."—*The New York Times Book Review*
0-394-72880-7 paper, $7.95

THE OGRE
by Michel Tournier, translated from the French by Barbara Bray

The story of a gentle giant's extraordinary experiences in World War II.

"Quite simply, a great novel."—*The New Yorker*
0-394-72407-0 paper, $8.95

NAPLES '44
by Norman Lewis

A young British intelligence officer's journal of his year in Allied-occupied Naples.

"An immensely gripping experience . . . a marvelous book."—S. J. Perelman
0-394-72300-7 paper, $7.95

THE WAR DIARIES: NOVEMBER 1939-MARCH 1940
by Jean-Paul Sartre, translated from the French by Quintin Hoare

Sartre's only surviving diaries: an intimate look at his life and thought at the beginning of World War II.

"An extraordinary book."—Alfred Kazin, *The Philadelphia Inquirer*
0-394-74422-5 paper, $10.95

A GUARD WITHIN
by Sarah Ferguson

The story of a young woman's heroic struggle to recover from a harrowing emotional breakdown.

"Overwhelming." —*The New York Times Book Review*

"A stunning and heroic achievement—reminds one of Sylvia Plath's last poems."
—*The Chicago Sun-Times*

0-394-75834-X paper, $7.95

ONCE IN EUROPA
(the second volume of the projected trilogy *Into Their Labors*)
by John Berger

A linked series of love stories, set among the peasants of Alpine France.

"Berger is one of our most gifted and imaginative contemporary writers [and] *Once in Europa* contains what may be his best writing to date."
—*The New York Times Book Review*

"Marvelous stories." —Angela Carter, *The Washington Post Book World*

0-394-75164-7 paper, $7.95

PIG EARTH
(the first volume of the projected trilogy *Into Their Labors*)
by John Berger

An exquisite fictional portrait of life in a small peasant village in the French Alps.

"Lovely, lyrical, haunting . . . a masterpiece." —Todd Gitlin, *The New Republic*

"A work of art." —*The Washington Post*

0-394-75739-4 paper, $7.95